BEWARE!!
DO NOT READ THIS
BOOK FROM
BEGINNING TO END!

Yes! You're psyched for your Tiki Island vacation. Then you go snorkeling — and a shark appears, looking for lunch!

If you hide from the shark in an underwater cave, you'll find a sunken ship — with a *real* skeleton crew. If you make one wrong move, you could become the newest crew member!

If you fight the shark with a sharp stone from the ocean floor, you learn that the stone has evil powers. You've got to get rid of it fast. But first you have to battle ghostly warriors and brave an active volcano!

You're in control of this scary adventure. You decide what will happen. And how terrifying the scares will be!

Start on PAGE 1. Then follow the instructions at the bottom of each page. *You* make the choices. If you choose well, you'll save Tiki Island from a terrible fate. But if you make the wrong choice . . . BEWARE!

SO TAKE A DEEP BREATH. CROSS YOUR FINGERS. AND TURN TO PAGE 1 TO *GIVE YOURSELF GOOSEBUMPS*!

READER BEWARE —
YOU CHOOSE THE SCARE!

Look for more
GIVE YOURSELF GOOSEBUMPS adventures
from R.L. STINE

R.L. STINE

GIVE YOURSELF

Goosebumps®

THE TWISTED TALE
OF TIKI ISLAND

AN
APPLE
PAPERBACK

SCHOLASTIC INC.
New York Toronto London Auckland
Sydney New Delhi Hong Kong

A PARACHUTE PRESS BOOK

ISBN-13: 978-0-590-93500-5

Copyright © 1997 by Parachute Press, Inc. All rights reserved. Published by Scholastic Inc. APPLE PAPERBACKS and the APPLE PAPERBACKS logo are registered trademarks of Scholastic Inc. GOOSEBUMPS is a registered trademark of Parachute Press, Inc.

This edition is for sale in Indian subcontinent only.

First Scholastic Printing, September 1997
Reprinted by Scholastic India Pvt. Ltd., March 2008
January; August 2010; November 2011; January 2012;
July; December 2013; August; December 2014;
August; November 2015

Printed at Shivam Offset Press, New Delhi

"Hurry up, Gina," you call to your cousin. The wooden dock creaks as you jump up and down. "The water's perfect for snorkeling."

"I'm coming! I'm coming!" Gina yells. "Yeow! I should have worn sandals. The sand is burning my feet."

You watch Gina hop across Tiki Island's famous white sand. Glancing around, you remember how much fun you had visiting the island last year.

Lucky for you, your mom is a travel writer. When she wrote about Tiki Island a year ago she brought your whole family. With Gina along this time, you know you're going to have a blast!

Gina jumps onto the dock to join you. She dumps her snorkeling gear next to yours. Then she gazes across the shimmering water. "Wow!" she gasps. "This place is amazing!"

A motorboat hums toward the dock. You've arranged for a ride to a nearby reef. You grin when you recognize the boy steering. It's Kala, the resort owner's son. He was your best buddy last year. "Hey, Kala!" you shout with a wave.

Kala ignores your greeting. And as the boat gets closer, you can see his face looks grim.

Turn to PAGE 2.

2

Kala noses the boat into the dock. He still hasn't said hello or even smiled at you.

"Kala!" you cry. "Don't you recognize me?"

Kala doesn't answer.

This is not the boy you remember. Last year he was a total goofball — always laughing and pulling pranks. Why is he so unfriendly now?

"What's up, Kala?" you ask. "Why are you acting so weird?"

Kala gazes at you a moment. "A curse has fallen on Tiki Island," he replies slowly. "No one is safe."

You stare at him. Then a wide grin spreads across your face. This must be one of Kala's practical jokes!

"Ignore him," you whisper to Gina. "He's just trying to scare us."

Gina rolls her eyes. "Whatever," she says. "Let's go check out the reef!"

You grab your snorkeling gear and jump into Kala's boat. "Oooh, I'm so scared of the curse," you tease him. "But I'll try to be brave."

"Don't make jokes," Kala says, frowning. "You may regret it."

Go to PAGE 3.

Kala turns his back on you and starts the motor.

As the boat flies over the crystal-clear water, you try to forget about Kala's odd behavior. Minutes later, you arrive at the reef and Kala cuts the engine.

"Take care to make wise choices while you are here," he warns you. "The curse of Tiki Island affects these surrounding waters. People have been known to . . . *disappear*."

"Maybe they disappear because you're so unfriendly!" you grumble. "Come on, Gina. The vacation officially begins now!"

Kala drops anchor. You and Gina put on your diving masks and snorkel mouthpieces and jump overboard. Both of you are good swimmers. You head toward the farthest point of the reef.

You glance back at Kala in the boat. His last words worry you. Could there really be a curse? You have noticed there are fewer tourists on Tiki Island this year. And people at the resort *have* been acting strangely. You hate to admit it, but you feel a little scared. "We should stick together," you tell Gina.

"Deal," she agrees.

You feel better.

Sort of.

Go to PAGE 27.

4

Wow, you think as you watch the shark's retreat. That was really weird.

But you're safe!

You turn the piece of stone over in your hand. It's a small triangle. One side is plain white. On the other side, a painted eye stares at you. Its deep, black pupil is surrounded by a purple ring. For a moment you feel hypnotized.

As you examine the triangle, it grows warm in your hand. You tuck it into your bathing suit. You'll figure out what it is later. After your close encounter with the shark, all you want to do is get back to the boat. And back on land!

Gina's head pops out of the water near the cave entrance. As you swim toward her, the stone piece begins to burn.

Where it touches you, your skin feels as if it's on fire!

Go to PAGE 63.

You and Gina race out of Hooahtoo's shack, leaving the Eye on the floor. The last thing you need is some weird stone with a curse on it! Let Hooahtoo return it!

"The eye shall be on you wherever you go!" Hooahtoo calls after you. "Beware!"

"I'd rather 'beware' than be there," Gina mutters.

The two of you don't slow down until you're far from Hooahtoo's shack. "I'm glad you left the Tiki Eye in the shack," Gina tells you. "Good riddance to bad rubbish."

"Yeah," you agree, jogging beside her. "That thing was nothing but bad luck from the moment I found it."

"Well, it's Hooahtoo's problem now," Gina says with a laugh.

But then her laughter turns into a shriek.

"What is it?" you cry, freezing in place.

She points at you. "I . . . I . . ." she stammers.

"You what?" you shout back at her.

"Not *I*," Gina sputters. "*EYE!* The eye! Look!" She points at your left shoe.

It's the eye! Sitting on the toe of your sneaker!

"Nooo!" you wail.

Shake a leg over to PAGE 102.

You're suffocating! Drowning! You have to breathe!

You burst through the surface of the water. You spit the snorkel out of your mouth.

"*PWAHHH!*" you gasp at last. You can breathe again!

You glance around. The current carried you and Gina through an opening and into a small pool in a high-ceilinged cave. A rocky staircase is carved into the wall.

The powerful current still pulls you toward the far end of the pool. But now that you can breathe again, you feel relieved.

Until you hear the sound of rushing water.

"Gina?" you call. Your voice echoes strangely in the watery cave. "Do you hear —"

"Help!" Gina shrieks ahead of you. "A waterfall!"

Oh, no! She's right!

The current drags you and Gina to the very edge of a giant waterfall. The foamy white water rushes downward.

You and Gina rush with it!

"*Aaaaaaaaahhhh!*" you scream as you plummet down, down, down. . . .

All the way down to PAGE 137.

Captain Bones knocks the barrels down with a bare-boned arm. The skeletons on the deck cheer as their Master shoves you toward the closet.

CLICK!

You're locked in with Gina!

It's pitch-black inside. And the tiny space stinks! You try not to breathe. You can feel Gina next to you. You can't see a thing, but you know she's tied up and gagged.

"Ssshhh," you whisper to her. "Don't make a sound. I'll untie you."

Your fingers fumble with the knots. It's too difficult in the dark. You remember there's a snorkeling flashlight hooked to the belt around your waist.

You could turn it on and see the knots better. But the light might catch the attention of the skeleton crew.

If you decide you really need light, turn to PAGE 68.

If you decide the light is too dangerous, don't turn it on, but do turn to PAGE 20.

A red-hot wave of flowing lava washes over you and Gina.

"*AAAHHHHhhhh!*" you and Gina scream together.

Until your mouths fill up with molten rock.

You're sucked under the thick, swirling, scalding sludge.

Oh, well. You got swept away by this tropical adventure. But you tried your best. And at least you had a *lava*-ly time — until you met this red-hot

END.

When the Tiki warriors see the one-eyed mask, they gasp. But before anyone can move, a powerful *KABOOM!* rocks the cavern. A blast of purple smoke explodes out of one wall.

As the smoke clears, the wall of stone slides open. An underground prison is revealed — filled with people you know!

"There's Tao, from the snack bar!" you whisper to Gina. "And there's Angela and Teeko, from the the dock. I know them!"

"Are they prisoners?" Gina asks. "What's going on?"

All the smoke has cleared now. You strain to see who else you know in the crowd of prisoners. Then you draw in a sharp breath. You're so upset, you forget to whisper. "There's Kala!" you shout.

Uh-oh.

Hooahtoo may be blind, but his hearing is excellent.

Turn to PAGE 116.

TAILS it is!

You follow the signs deep into the jungle. The narrow path is covered with vines and thick roots. "They sure don't make it easy to get there!" you grumble, tripping on a root.

You finally reach the archaeological site. You wonder how to find Dr. Oates. You approach a young man who is tying a string around a staked-out square of earth.

"Excuse us," you begin. "Can you tell us where to find Dr. Oates?"

"That's him," he tells you, pointing to a small, scruffy-looking man in khakis and a safari hat. Dr. Oates is yelling at a worker in a language you can't understand. The worker seems scared.

Dr. Oates doesn't seem very friendly. Or in a very good mood. "Maybe this was a mistake," you whisper to Gina. "Maybe we should have listened to Kala and gone to see Hooahtoo instead."

"Maybe we should look around on our own," Gina whispers back.

If you decide to go see Hooahtoo, turn to PAGE 81.

If you explore the camp on your own, turn to PAGE 73.

If you stick to your plan and approach Dr. Oates, go to PAGE 51.

Great job! You escaped from the octopuses! And with only a few dozen purple spots left on your skin by the suckers.

You leave the octopuses tangled in their own arms and swim back to the sunken ship. You'll just have to help Gina all by yourself. This time you're careful to avoid any sea creatures. You spot a few schools of fish, but they ignore you.

When you reach the ship, you swim to the gun port and gaze into the cabin where Gina was tied up.

She's gone!

Where did the pirate skeletons take her?

Now you definitely have to sneak on board.

Go to PAGE 112.

You're right-handed. So you press your hand into the right handprint.

"Gina!" you exclaim excitedly. "It's opening!"

The door swings open into a dark room. A hole in the high ceiling lets in a dim yellow light. You and Gina dart inside. The door swings shut in the faces of the two Tiki warriors

"That was close!" you gasp.

"We escaped!" Gina cheers. You and Gina slap high fives. Then you slide down to the floor, exhausted.

"Yikes!" you shriek. Something is crawling all over you! You leap to your feet.

Lizards! Dozens of lizards scurry to get out of your way. Their red tongues lash out at you as they run over your legs and arms. "Lava lizards!" you cry. "They're all over this place!"

"Gross!" Gina squeals, shaking off the scaly monsters.

Now you see that the lizards aren't the only strange things in this room.

Get an eyeful on PAGE 103.

Of course you turn down the offer! You have a feeling this bit of stone might be priceless.

"Thanks, but no thanks," you tell Dr. Oates. "But Gina and I will help you search for other stuff around here!"

The archaeologist frowns. "It's dangerous in these jungles," he warns. "I've already lost several of my workers. There are spirits here. And they don't want us trespassing!"

You remember Kala's warning about people disappearing. You look at Gina and mouth, "The curse!"

"Are you sure you won't reconsider my offer?" Dr. Oates asks. "I'm prepared to go even higher."

But before he can tell you how much more he'd pay, you hear someone shouting in the jungle. "Dr. Oates!" a voice cries. "Help!"

Dr. Oates runs to the edge of the jungle. He stops suddenly. "Stay back!" he shouts to you and Gina. He turns to face you.

His face is white as a sheet.

He looks as if he's just seen a ghost!

Go to PAGE 100.

"Take us up to the top," the loudmouth shouts. "We're not scared of a little noise. It'll be years before —"

An even louder rumble drowns out the big mouth. That's all it takes to terrify most of the tourists. They scatter, running toward the village.

But the tour guide remains. And the loudmouth heads up the path to the top of Kenalua.

Is he going up to the mouth of the volcano? you wonder. He's either really brave or really dumb.

But maybe you should follow him. After all, Hooahtoo told you to break the spell by bringing the Tiki Eye to the volcano. And he warned you not to waste any time.

Or should you wait to see what the tour guide does?

After all, she's the expert!

If you follow the loudmouth up the volcano, turn to PAGE 109.

If you wait to see what the tour guide does, turn to PAGE 31.

"We'll just see about that, Mr. Hooahtoo!" you shout at the tiny bearded Tiki leader. You pick up a rock and aim it right at Hooahtoo's forehead.

He shields himself with the Tiki mask. The rock bounces off the mask. It smashes down onto a set of remote-control buttons built into the armrest of his throne.

Instantly, another blast of purple smoke pours out of the prison wall.

"The rock!" you gasp. "It activated the controls!"

To the prisoners' amazement and your surprise, the steel bars of the prison rise up.

Your rock hit the button that opens the bars!

Turn to PAGE 86

You stay right where you are. You're afraid if you move, they'll see you. And you remember something Hooahtoo said.

"Hooahtoo warned us about this," you whisper. "Remember, he said we have to pass a wall of Tiki warriors. Maybe we have to get by them to lift the curse."

Another shaft of lightning crackles overhead. In the brief flash of light you see symbols of suns, moons, and arrows burned into the arms and legs of the two warriors. You also see something that startles you.

"Their medallions!" you gasp.

"I see them," Gina murmurs.

The Tiki warriors both wear medallions exactly like Hooahtoo's! Decorated with the Tiki Eye.

Exactly like the eye burned into your hand!

And now the piece of stone in your pocket is growing warmer. You can feel it right through the straw box.

Turn to PAGE 53.

"Climb back up the steps!" you shout to Gina. "It's our only chance!"

You lead the way up the steps. Only three of the rotted wood stairs are above the water. You huddle close to the ceiling and try to keep your legs away from the meat-eating fish.

SNAP! The top step breaks in two! You fall to the next step down.

SNAP! The next step breaks! You drop to the one below.

SNAP! The last step cracks in half. You drop into the waiting jaws of the hungry fish.

It's over in seconds. The fish waste no time in finishing you and Gina off. All that's left are your bones.

But don't worry. You won't be alone. As a matter of fact, you'll fit right in! There's a whole crowd waiting on deck to welcome you to Captain Bones's skeleton crew.

THE END

You don't want to wait to find out who — or what — is coming. You reach for the secret door, knocking over a large Tiki mask. It gives you an idea.

"Here, Gina," you hiss. "Put this on." You hand Gina the mask. Then you grab one for yourself. Once the masks are in place, you shove open the door.

The Tiki warriors stand by the fire. They still clutch the nasty-looking branding tools. As you and Gina step through the door, the warriors glance at you.

"*AAiiiiieee!*" one of the warriors cries. He drops to the ground! The other takes one look in your direction and runs screaming from the cave!

You smile under your mask. "It worked!" you declare. "We scared them off with the masks!"

"I wonder why these masks scared them so much," Gina comments.

You shrug. "Who cares!" you reply. "As long as it worked."

You reach up to pull off the mask. As you do, a movement behind you catches your eye.

You whirl around.

And scream!

Turn to PAGE 87.

The man with the big voice is actually tiny!
Teeny-tiny!

Hooahtoo barely comes up to your chest!

A long white beard flows down the front of his purple robe. Seashells and purple flowers crown his mane of white hair. The purple mist continues to swirl around him. You can't figure out where it's coming from.

Then Hooahtoo stares right at you. There is no color in his eyes. They are as white as his hair.

Hooahtoo is blind.

"Show me the thing you have brought with you," Hooahtoo orders again. He stretches his hand toward you.

As you stare at him, your eyes are drawn to a medallion hanging around his neck. In the center of the medallion is a jeweled eye.

You've seen an eye exactly like it before.

On the gleaming stone piece you found on the ocean floor!

Go to PAGE 36.

You decide it's too risky to turn on the flashlight. In total darkness you keep working on Gina's ropes. "I got it!" you whisper excitedly.

"Oh, thank goodness!" Gina cries as you pull off her gag. "They're monsters. I heard them talking. They're planning to come back from the dead and take over the whole island!"

"Is that possible?" you ask.

"Yes! The only thing stopping them before was that they didn't know the way up. Now we're here — and they want us to lead them! If we refuse, we're finished."

"And if we don't refuse?" you ask.

"Then Tiki Island and everyone on it is finished," Gina whispers.

Go to PAGE 119.

"He's free," Dr. Oates declares. "Finally, the spirit of the Tiki King is free. Thanks to you."

The three of you stroll back to Dr. Oates's camp. "You will become a part of this island's history," Dr. Oates tells you. "As a reward I'll give you each a Tiki mask to take home. The islanders would want you to have them for lifting the curse."

You and Gina carry your masks proudly. You thank Dr. Oates and head back toward the jungle path.

Oooops! You trip on a root. You stumble and knock Gina down. You both land hard, shattering your masks into a zillion pieces.

From the pile of pieces, two new ghosts arise.

Yup. Two. One for each mask.

You'll go down in Tiki history all right. As the clumsy jerks who lifted the Tiki curse — and then started it all over again.

In duplicate.

Double trouble, pal.

Well, maybe the Tiki Islanders won't be TWO mad at you.

But, you realize, that may be TWO much to hope for in

THE END.

THE END.

22

You're going to the mouth of the volcano.

The giant lizard is carrying you and Gina to the very top of Kenalua Mountain.

The lizard steps out of the tunnel into fresh air. Gina gasps behind you. "Look how high we are!" she exclaims. "We must be near the top!"

The lizard comes to an abrupt stop. It practically dumps you and Gina onto the ground. Then it nudges you from behind.

"Okay! Okay!" you cry. "I'm going! *Sheeesh!*"

You and Gina climb the rest of the way. To the very top of Kenalua Mountain. Right to the walkway that runs along the mouth of the volcano.

"Well, here goes," you declare. You take the stone piece out of your pocket. You glance back at the giant lizard. It almost seems to nod.

Then you rear back and hurl the Tiki Eye into the heart of the volcano!

Turn to PAGE 82.

You decide to go back through the tunnel and try to get help. There are just too many of them to fight on your own.

You dash into the mouth of the tunnel. As soon as you cross the threshold, the entrance snaps shut!

You turn and gaze at the blocked passage. Strange gleaming growths hang in front of the entrance to the tunnel. They look just like teeth!

And the ground beneath your feet has changed. It's not the sparkling beach of the lagoon. It's soft and pinkish.

Whoops! Wrong tunnel!

In fact, this isn't a tunnel at all. It's the throat of some sea monster you've never even seen! And never will, come to think of it.

A loud gurgling comes from farther down the throat. You feel everything vibrate and shake. The creature is swallowing! You're being sucked down. Down into the belly of the beast!

GULP!

Too bad the last meal of this vacation turned out to be YOU.

THE END

You decide you'd better pretend to get rid of the stone. Before Gina has a fit!

"Okay, Gina," you agree. "I'll chuck this thing." You reach into your pocket and pretend to pull out the piece of stone. You act as if you're throwing as hard as you can.

"Wow!" Gina exclaims. "Awesome pitch! I can't even see where it went. Now let's get out of here!" Then she turns and races down the mountain path.

You suddenly feel bad about lying to your cousin. And afraid of what might happen if you don't follow Hooahtoo's directions.

"Gina, wait!" you call. "I didn't really —"

You dash after her. You need to convince her to go up to the mouth of the volcano to break the curse.

"Gina!" you call again. She darts around a curve in the path.

When you round the corner, Gina is nowhere in sight.

She's vanished!

Go look for her on PAGE 38.

25

You hear Gina's muffled cries from inside the closet. You feel so helpless. If you could just open that closet and . . .

A bony hand gripping your shoulder interrupts your thoughts.

"I've found the other one!" a scratchy voice bellows.

You whirl around.

And stand nose to nose with the biggest skeleton of all!

Only he *has* no nose! Just a gaping hole.

You gasp in the face of this walking horror show.

"Allow me to introduce myself," snarls the fleshless creature. "I am the Master of the Ship, Captain Bones! And you are about to join my crew!"

Go to PAGE 7.

Hooahtoo, that's who!

"What's he doing here?" you cry.

"And where did all that treasure come from?" Gina adds.

Suddenly, the drums stop beating. Hooahtoo stands. He turns his head in your direction. You and Gina duck away from the edge.

Did he sense your presence? You know he doesn't need his eyes to see! Your heart pounds so hard, it sounds as if the drums have started up again!

You hear Hooahtoo address the crowd. "I am Hooahtoo!" roars the tiny white-haired man. "When the Tiki Eye has been returned to the sacred Tiki Mask, I shall be supreme ruler of Tiki Island. All the power of the island spirits shall belong to me! Those who are with me shall live. Those who are against me shall be sealed in my underground prison. *Forever*!"

Oh, no! Hooahtoo told you to trust no one. You never thought that warning included him!

You and Gina crawl back to the edge of the ledge. You have to see what Hooahtoo is doing! You stare down.

Hooahtoo holds up a jeweled and golden Tiki mask.

And it's missing one eye!

Go to PAGE 9.

This part of the reef is shallow. You and Gina float above brightly colored fish that dart around the coral.

Gina taps you on the shoulder. She points to an opening in the reef. An undersea cave! She wants to explore it.

You're about to follow her, when you catch sight of something gleaming on the reef floor. What could it be? you wonder. It's as big as your fist and comes to a sharp point. Cool! Maybe it's a spearhead.

Gina's already swimming toward the cave. You pop your head out of the water and see Kala waving and yelling from the boat. It's too soon to head back, you think. What does Kala want?

Then you see it. A dark fin slicing through the water. Kala was trying to warn you.

It's a shark!

And it's heading straight for you!

What should you do? Try to swim into the cave? Or should you grab the spearheadlike thing and use it to protect yourself?

Quick! Make up your mind!

If you swim toward the cave in the reef, go to PAGE 111.

If you dive for the gleaming spearhead, turn to PAGE 40.

"I'm waiting for an explanation, you little brat!" Dr. Oates bellows. His loud voice wakens Gina.

"What's going on?" she cries.

You frantically search your pockets. "It's gone!" you wail. "I've lost the stone piece!"

"Get out of here!" Dr. Oates shouts. "And don't bother me again!"

You and Gina take off. You dart through the archaeological dig. You trip and stumble through the jungle, all the way to the resort.

You and Gina lean against a tree, catching your breath. "Thank goodness we got out of there," you say, panting. "And I never want to hear another word about that stupid stone eye again!"

Gina nods. "You won't hear about it from me," she promises.

You notice a crowd of reporters on the front lawn of the hotel. "Hey, what do you suppose that's all about?" you ask Gina.

She shrugs. "Let's see," she says.

Mingle with the crowd on PAGE 42.

You and Gina quickly change out of your wet bathing suits in the dockside cabanas. You carry the stone piece wrapped in your towel. You don't want it to burn you again! Then you head into town.

You pass a sign by the side of the road. "Check that out," you tell Gina. You point at the crudely lettered notice.

"Visit the archaeological dig!" she reads aloud. "See ancient artifacts, explained by Dr. Oliver Oates!"

"Dr. Oates," you repeat. "Maybe that's who we should see about the stone eye."

"Yeah," Gina agrees. "Maybe the thing you found is an ancient artifact. Then Dr. Oates would know all about it."

"After all," you add, "I don't even know this Hooahtoo guy."

"Well, you don't know Dr. Oates, either," Gina points out. "If you ask me, it's a toss-up."

She's right. It *is* a toss-up. So toss it up!

Toss up a coin. If it lands on HEADS, go see Hooahtoo on PAGE 81.

If the coin lands on TAILS, go see Oates on PAGE 10.

"It's a deal!" you tell Dr. Oates. "You give us two hundred dollars, and we give you the Tiki Eye."

"Wise choice," he murmurs. He reaches into his pocket, pulls out two hundred-dollar bills and tosses them at you. The bills flutter to the ground.

Then he snatches the stone piece. "Now take the money and get out of here," Dr. Oates orders. "I've got work to do!" With that, he spins around and heads into the shack. You and Gina pick up the money and head back to the path.

"I'm going straight to the Swim Shop!" Gina declares. She waves her hundred-dollar bill at you. "I see a new bathing suit, some flippers, and maybe an underwater radio in my future!"

You can't resist one last glance at the archaeological site.

You gasp when your eyes land on a strange figure in the doorway of the shack. It's Dr. Oates. You recognize his clothes. Only now he also wears a huge Tiki mask! It matches the one he showed you in the book!

A worker glances up from where he is digging. His eyes meet the eyes of the mask. Instantly, the worker keels over into the hole. Another worker looks up. As soon as she sees the mask she too crumples to the ground, moaning.

"The mask!" you whisper hoarsely to Gina. "They're terrified of the mask!"

Run to PAGE 96.

The volcano's rumbling grows louder. You watch the tour guide. Why is everyone running except her? you wonder.

You turn toward Gina. Her face is white with fear. You grab her sleeve as she starts to run. "Wait," you urge her.

You pull Gina behind a thick clump of bushes. You put a finger to your lips. She nods.

The tour guide pushes aside a shrub. She yanks out a tape recorder and shuts it off. Instantly, the mountain stops rumbling.

"It worked!" she calls. "The volcano recording frightened them away." She laughs as she tears off her tour guide badge and throws it on the ground.

The loudmouthed guy jogs back down the mountain to join her. "Well done," he congratulates the fake tour guide. "We must keep all outsiders away from the Tiki altar!"

They reach down into the bushes. Night is falling, so it's hard to see what they're doing. You motion Gina to follow you. You creep out from your hiding place for a better look.

A flash of lightning cracks across the sky. In that flash the tour guide and the loudmouthed guy turn to face you. Only now they look very different.

And very terrifying.

Go to PAGE 62.

Luckily for you, the skeleton guards don't seem to see you. They peer into the water with blank stares.

You swim to the surface and gulp in air. You see gun ports spaced along the side of the ship above the waterline. You swim to the closest one and peek in — there's a cabin with a table and four chairs. Skeletons sit in three of the chairs.

Gina is tied into the fourth chair! She's blindfolded and gagged.

Your best friend is a prisoner of the skeleton crew!

You have to think fast. Should you swim around to the other side of the ship and sneak on board? Or should you try to get back to Kala and his boat and bring help?

If you sneak aboard the ship, turn to PAGE 112.

If you try to get back to Kala and bring help, turn to PAGE 75.

You have no time to wrestle with a stalagmite. You'll try the Tiki Eye. Maybe you can use it to bargain for your life. Or jab the warriors if they come too close.

You yank the stone piece out of your pocket.

"Tiki Eye!" one of the warriors cries. He aims his spear at you and lunges.

"No!" Gina shrieks.

Terror makes you feel like everything is happening in slow motion. You stand frozen. Staring at the gleaming spear point. Holding out the Tiki Eye. Then you see something strange.

The eye is glowing purple!

You snap out of it — because the warrior's spear is an inch away from you!

Your mouth opens in a silent scream.

Then the spear seems to bounce off an invisible wall!

The purple glow of the Tiki Eye is acting as a protective shield!

The warrior tries again. But his spear can't get through the Tiki force field.

You don't know how long the eye's protective power will last. You have to figure out your next step!

See what it is on PAGE 126.

The impact makes you dizzy. The walls spin. Your head pounds.

No. It isn't your head that's pounding.

It's the sound of drums!

You sit up slowly and glance around. You're on a ledge overlooking a huge cavern. Below, a fire blazes in a circle around a golden throne. Your heart skips a beat at the sight of the hundreds of masked warriors surrounding the throne. All of them carry sharp spears.

Gina's out cold on the floor next to you. "Gina?" you whisper, nudging her. "Gina! Wake up!"

"Huh?" Gina sits up groggily. "Where are we?"

"I'm not sure," you tell her. The two of you peer down from the ledge. "Whoa," you mutter. "Check that out!"

Chests full of treasure line the aisle leading to the throne. Golden goblets, coins, rubies, emeralds, and diamonds spill onto the floor.

You hear Gina gasp.

"What is it?" you ask.

"Isn't he — isn't he — ?" Gina sputters.

"Isn't he WHO????" you demand.

Turn to PAGE 26 to find out.

"Why don't you ask the scoundrel on the floor!" Dr. Oates suggests. You help him scramble out of the trunk. He shakes the ropes off his wrists. "He should have the answers for you!"

Gina gets off the person you *thought* was Dr. Oates. The real Dr. Oates roughly turns the guy over.

"Kala!" you cry in surprise. "You?"

Kala ignores you. He just lies on the floor, gazing unblinkingly at the ceiling.

"As soon as I set the eye into the mask," Dr. Oates explains, "Kala jumped me and shoved me into the trunk. He must have dressed in clothes like mine and covered his face with the mask."

"But why?" you ask your former friend. "How could you have become so evil?"

Go to PAGE 113.

You have the pointy stone wrapped in your towel. Hooahtoo points to the bundle. "Show me what's in there," he orders.

"How does he see it?" Gina whispers.

You shrug, then kneel down. As you unroll the towel, Hooahtoo leans forward. Slowly, he waves his wrinkled hand over the towel. His hand stops directly over the stone piece. It's as if he sees with his hand instead of his eyes.

His bony fingers touch the broken stone piece lightly. When he feels the painted eye, he throws his arms up and shrieks. You're so startled, you stumble backwards.

"The curse is on you!" he shouts. "The curse is on you!"

"This guy's been in the purple mist too long," Gina mutters. "Let's get out of here."

Maybe Gina's right. Hooahtoo is really weird.

Hooahtoo seems to read your mind. "If you go, the curse goes with you," he warns. "If you stay, the curse shall be broken."

There's no way you're staying here one second longer. Curse or no curse, you're getting out!

If you grab the bit of stone and race for the door, run to PAGE 91.

If you leave the stone behind, dash to PAGE 5.

The ghost is getting way too close!

"Try to remember how the legend says we can escape," you beg Dr. Oates.

"I'm trying," Dr. Oates says. He seems frozen to his spot. "I think the legend says if you stare into the ghost's eyes, you'll defeat him."

"That's easy!" you exclaim. What a relief! You can definitely survive this encounter!

"Wait!" Dr. Oates cries. "Maybe the legend says if you gaze into his eyes, you're lost for sure."

You and Gina stare at the terrified archaeologist.

He's no help! you think. And he's supposed to be the expert!

The ghost is only a few feet away. And it's floating toward you! What are you going to do? How will you decide?

If you have blue or green eyes, stare into the ghost's eyes on PAGE 43.

If you have any other color eyes, avoid the ghost's eyes on PAGE 72.

"Gina?" you yell. "Where are you?"

No answer.

You peer up and down the path. It's empty.

"Come on, Gina," you holler. "Quit kidding around!"

Now you're getting annoyed. "Gina!" you shout. "Why won't you answer me?"

It would serve her right if you just left. Or played a trick on her!

On the other hand, Kala did say people disappear. Maybe you should search for her.

If you decide to teach Gina a lesson, turn to PAGE 129.

If you do a thorough search, turn to PAGE 78.

You take out the Tiki Eye and place it in Dr. Oates's hand. "Here," you whisper. "He needs this a whole lot more than I do."

"Look out!" Gina cries suddenly. "The ghost!"

You jump as a ghostly arm reaches for the stone piece in Dr. Oates's hand. You're so freaked out, you fall over. The archaeologist keeps his head down, but sticks out his open palm.

A strong wind whips around the three of you. Trees rustle. Birds squawk.

And then there is silence.

When Dr. Oates pulls his hand back, the Tiki Eye is gone.

And so is the ghost warrior.

Turn to PAGE 21.

With the shark closing in, defending yourself seems like your best choice. You take a deep breath and dive below the surface. You race toward the gleaming object.

You pick it up. Oh, no! It's not a spearhead! It's just a piece of brightly painted stone.

But it *is* sharp. And it's better than nothing!

You surface and gulp air. Kala is pulling up the anchor, but he'll never get to you in time. Gina is nowhere in sight. The shark's fin cuts through the water, streaking toward you.

Closer. Closer.

Fear clutches your heart as tightly as you clutch the stone. Will it pierce the shark's tough skin?

The shark is so close, you can count its teeth! You paddle in place and hold the stone high, ready to slam it into the beast's face.

To your surprise, the shark freezes, its mouth wide open and its teeth gleaming. It rolls on its side. One black eye stares at the stone.

Then the creature turns and flees!

Go to PAGE 4.

The two of you stare at the giant reptile.

"Is it asleep?" Gina whispers.

"I don't think so. I think the eye has some kind of power over it," you explain.

"How can we make sure?" Gina asks.

"I'm going to try something," you tell her. "I just hope it works." You reach a trembling hand out to the lizard. It doesn't budge. Carefully, gently, you stroke the lizard's scaly back.

Maybe you're crazy, but you could swear the big guy just smiled!

"He seems to like you!" Gina exclaims.

No doubt about it. You continue to pet the gigantic lizard. It rolls over like a big dog, wanting its tummy rubbed.

Gina giggles. "I can't believe I was so afraid of him," she says. "He's harmless."

"Don't be so sure," you caution her. "I think he's only harmless because of the Tiki Eye. But," you continue, "I also think he can help us get out of here!"

Turn to PAGE 92.

You and Gina walk toward the crowd.

You spot your mom nearby. She waves you over. "Where have you been?" she asks. "You missed all the excitement. Someone found an ancient artifact! And it may be worth millions!"

You gulp. "Millions?" you repeat. "Of dollars?"

Your mom nods. "Some kind of eye that's been missing from a ceremonial mask."

Eye? Did she say *"eye"*?

Eye-yi-yi!

"Apparently a man named Hooahtoo offered a substantial reward for its return," your mom continues. "And some tourist stumbled over it walking through the jungle." She sighs. "Too bad one of us didn't find it!" She winks at you and Gina.

"Yeah," you mutter. "Too bad."

"What's the matter, hon?" your mom asks. "You look funny. Are you feeling sick?"

You bet you are! Imagine all that money — so near, and yet so far. You came so close to being a millionaire, you could almost taste it. And then it all vanished.

In the blink of an eye.

THE END

No way are you shutting your eyes with a twelve-foot ghost warrior just a few feet away from you.

You've heard with certain animals, the best defense is to stay still and stare at them. Maybe it will work with the ghost.

You gaze directly into the ghost's eyes.

"What are you looking at, shorty?" the ghost snaps at you. "Haven't your parents told you it's impolite to stare?"

Huh?

"You are a very rude child," the ghost scolds. "And you need to be taught a lesson."

Suddenly everything around you vanishes. The jungle, Gina, Dr. Oates — all gone. Instead, you find yourself surrounded by thick books.

You grab one. Dust flies from the cover, making you sneeze. You brush off the cover and read the title. *Good Manners for Bad Children.* Yikes!

You glance at the other books. They are all etiquette books — books on being polite.

Oh, well. You're going to be the most polite kid in the world. Because you have all of eternity to learn every rule there is — thank you very much!

THE END

RUMBLE!

You have to warn them, or you'll all be buried alive in diamonds!

"STOP!" you shout. "STOP!"

They're laughing so loud, they can't hear you. Now Gina joins in. "STOP!" she yells. "STOP! STOP! STOP!"

Together you shout your very loudest. "STOP!"

RUMBLE!

RUMBLE!

RUMBLE!

RUMBLE!

RUMBLE!

Hurry! Go to PAGE 83!

Now the skeleton beside you screams too.

It *is* Gina! You would recognize her yell anywhere!

But why is she calling the pirate skeletons?

Then the horrible answer hits you. Gina, your own cousin, has betrayed you. She's turning you over to the enemy!

You hear their bony feet clacking on the wooden deck as the skeleton pirates run to the closet. The door flies open. Now you see clearly. The tattered cloth is the remains of Gina's bathing suit. And that smirking expression on the bony skull is definitely Gina's.

There's no doubt about it. The screaming skeleton beside you is your cousin! She has become one of them.

And soon you'll be one of them too.

"The spell of the pink crystals always works that way," the Captain cackles. "Anyone who stays too long in the glow of the crystal joins us. It's your time now."

Gina lays a bony arm around you. "Cheer up," she tells you. "We wanted this vacation to last forever. Now it will."

THE END

You glance down from the rocky rim of the small pool at the top of the stairs. Most of the skeletons are too busy fighting to notice you've escaped.

But not Captain Bones.

"They're gone!" he shouts. "The kids are gone!"

Captain Bones clatters to the stairs, followed by his two remaining loyal crew members. They try to follow you up the stone staircase. But bones have no traction. Their bony feet slip on the steps. Like a row of toppling dominoes, they fall backwards down the stairs.

Screaming and bellowing, Captain Bones begs for help. "After them! Tiki Island belongs to us! The treasure is ours!"

But it's no use. The battling skeletons ignore him.

You and Gina make your way along the narrow stone ledge along the side of the pool. This time the currents are on your side. The path is clear. Dragging the trunk between you, you surface.

There's no shark there now. But Kala, his father, and your parents are waiting for you in boats anchored by the reef.

Go to PAGE 128.

You search the tunnel for Gina. When you walk back a few feet, you discover another tunnel. Maybe Gina went that way.

"Gina?" you cry. "Gina? Are you in here?"

Gina doesn't answer. But you hear sounds coming from farther down the tunnel.

You run toward the sound. After a few yards, the tunnel curves left — then opens into a large cave. Sparkling lights blind you. You throw your arms over your face to shield your eyes from the blaze.

You move your arms away and squint. It takes a minute to adjust to the brightness. But then your eyes widen in amazement!

This cave is actually a lagoon. Strange plants loom overhead. The lights are not lights at all. They're shimmering crystals — pink, yellow, blue. They cover the beach and the rock walls surrounding the lagoon. The colors dazzle you. Then you realize — the crystals are more than just colorful rocks.

They're diamonds!

You gaze in awe at the sparkling surroundings. Then you remind yourself why you're here.

"Gina?" you call out in a loud whisper.

A sudden whip-crack snaps in the air.

Jump! Then jump over to PAGE 115.

Tickle a crowd of giant octopuses under their arms?

Are you serious?

These octopuses are monsters! They're dangerous! They want to wrap you up so tightly, you can't even breathe!

Did you really think you could get out of this octopus mess just by tickling them?

You've got to be kidding!

But go ahead and try it if you like.

When you find yourself still wrapped in the arms of danger, turn to PAGE 121 for some serious escape tactics!

Hooahtoo gives you and Gina detailed directions to the volcano. He warns you to trust no one. "Do not be deceived by face or form," he advises. "Do not be fooled. Even by your own eyes."

"I don't like this whole thing," Gina whispers nervously to you. "Is he for real?"

"What is real and what is not real is for me to know and you to find out," Hooahtoo answers for you. "You must go now. There is no time to lose."

The tiny old blind man picks up the Tiki Eye and places it inside a box made of woven grass. "Here," he says, handing you the box. "Take this and go. Now! And remember: As long as you have the eye, you are in danger."

Turn to PAGE 84.

You press your left hand hard onto the handprint.

But the wall doesn't move. Instead, the floor beneath your feet drops away! You and Gina plummet down through the hole.

"Oh, no-o-o-o-o-o-o-o!" you both shriek. You're sliding down a shaft inside Kenalua Volcano Mountain!

A blinding white-hot light blinds you. Waves of heat wash over you. A roaring furnace sound fills your ears. It's deafening!

You glance up. The two Tiki warriors bend over the hole far above you. They gaze down at you. They shout and point excitedly, but you don't understand what they're saying.

You glance down.

"No!" you gasp.

A sea of molten lava bubbles and smokes below you.

You're whooshing straight toward the boiling core of Kenalua!

Fall to PAGE 107.

You decide to ask Dr. Oates about the stone piece. You step forward and clear your throat. "We came to get information about this," you explain. You open the towel and reveal the strange painted eye. "I found it when we were snorkeling."

Dr. Oates's eyes widen. He bends over and brings his face close to the stone.

"The weird thing is," you continue, "I held it up to a shark, and —"

But Dr. Oates doesn't allow you to finish your sentence. "Shhhh! Shhhh!" he hushes you. He examines the piece with great interest.

"Wait here," he orders you.

He dashes to his tent and comes back carrying a thick book. He flips to a page showing a giant Tiki mask. He holds the picture next to the stone.

Your piece matches the right eye of the mask!

Turn to PAGE 134.

Yes! You remember a shark swimming toward you.

But you also remember how you scared away the shark before. You held up the broken piece of stone you found. It made the shark turn and swim away.

That's what you'll do now, you think. You'll scare him away with the broken stone piece.

The shark comes closer and closer. His jaws are opening wide.

The stone piece! Where is it?

Sorry.

But you wished and wished and wished you'd never found it. Guess what? Your wish came true.

Bad luck for you, good luck for the shark!

THE END

The warriors still haven't noticed you. Maybe you should follow them. They might lead you up the volcano to the special Tiki mask. Then you can replace the eye and lift the curse.

The stone piece grows so warm in your pocket, it begins to burn. It's hurting your leg. You can't stand it anymore!

"*Yeeeeeoooowwwwww!*" you cry out.

As soon as you scream, the Tiki warriors whirl in your direction. They aim their spears at you.

"Run!" you scream.

You and Gina spin around and take off. But the warriors are too fast. Too strong. They grab you and Gina. They drag you kicking and screaming into a cave in the side of the mountain.

Once you are inside, the warriors speak. "Don't waste your energy fighting a battle you cannot win," one warrior grunts.

"There is no escape from the Kalookie Cave," the other warns. "And now we must get you ready to greet our great leader."

Go to PAGE 66.

"Wow!" Gina gasps. "Look at that! What is it?"

"A ship!" you cry. "An old shipwreck!"

You and Gina tread water and wait to see what happens. Once the ship fully rises, the red glow diminishes. The black water fades to a dark blue. Silence surrounds you.

"Come on," you whisper. "Let's get a closer look!"

Swimming toward the battered ship, you notice it tips to one side. A tattered flag with a skull and crossbones hangs limply from a broken pole. You have a clear view of the damaged wooden deck.

"Oh, my gosh!" Gina sputters. "A treasure chest! And it's full of treasure!"

A huge wooden chest lies open on deck. Gold pieces spill over its sides. More gold than you've ever seen, even in movies!

"I can't believe what we've found!" you murmur in amazement. "A real pirate ship, with a real treasure!"

A movement on deck distracts you from your discovery. A shadowy figure approaches. Your eyes widen as you realize who — or what — is staring down at you.

"*AAAhhhhh!*" you scream in horror. "It's a skeleton!"

Turn to PAGE 98.

Stones, sticks, and uprooted shrubs tear at your skin. You and Gina are caught in a tide of volcano debris spewing from the mouth of Kenalua.

With a deafening roar, the earth beneath you cracks open like an overripe melon! A force from inside the crack sucks in you and Gina.

With a loud *GULP*, the mountain swallows you both!

Your vacation is very suddenly, very definitely over.

You and Gina kick and scream in the stomach of the volcano. You grab hands and bounce around, trying to give the mountain indigestion. Your mother always taught you it was not polite to burp. But if only the volcano would do just that! One loud belch is all it would take to free you.

Anything to make the grumbling mountain erupt.

But your bouncing doesn't work. The mountain seems to think you taste fine.

Don't you wish you didn't have such good taste?

THE END

"But we don't know how to get out of here," you wail. "We got here by mistake!"

Captain Bones doesn't believe you. "Throw them into the brig!" he orders. "A few days aboard our ghost ship may change their minds!"

Gina squeezes your arm. "Let's just show them the waterfall," she whispers shakily. "Maybe they can figure out the rest."

You think of your mom and Kala and all the rest of the islanders who have always been so friendly in the past. This horrible skeleton man wants to destroy them all! If you show him the way out, you may be responsible for causing the worst disaster Tiki Island has ever known.

And if you refuse, you may never see daylight again.

What should you do?

If you decide to lead Captain Bones and his crew to the waterfall, turn to PAGE 101.

If you refuse, turn to PAGE 74.

Breathlessly, you run without looking back. Gina is panting and gasping. So are all the other islanders.

At last you reach the end of the tunnel. You stand in the mouth of a cave looking out at the ocean. You made it! You're safe!

Something sharp in your bathing suit jabs you. It's the piece of pink crystal you found. Taking it out, you hold it up to the sun. Through the crystal, everything looks rosy.

Then you remember. It's not just any old crystal. It's a diamond. It could be worth thousands of dollars!

You're rich!

Wow. Now things *really* look rosy!

THE END

"What's it doing?" Gina gasps. "Why is it standing there like that?"

You stare at the giant lizard. It stares back. It still doesn't move.

Then you realize it isn't staring at you. It's staring at your hand.

The hand with the image of the eye burned into it.

You test your theory. Very slowly, you wave your hand up and down. You watch the lizard's beady yellow eyes follow the path of the eye.

Then your mouth drops open in astonishment.

The giant lizard kneels down, laying its head at your feet!

Turn to PAGE 41.

Hey — you cheated! But you still won't make it through the tangled mess of octopuses' arms. They're squeezing you so tightly, you think you'll be crushed.

"Nooooooo!!!!" you scream in frustration. Then, because you can't think of anything better to do, you open your mouth wide. You chomp down hard on an octopus tentacle.

Bad idea.

You've heard that a vampire bite will make you a vampire, right? And if you're bitten by a were-wolf, well, you know the story.

It works the same way with an octopus. Only in reverse. Yup! It doesn't need to bite *you*. You just need to bite *it*!

Don't believe it? Glance down at your arm. Oops! I mean arms. Check out your big round head.

Face it. You've turned into a giant octopus!

All you were trying to do was lend Gina a hand. Now you don't have one to lend her! But your new group of friends welcomes you with open arms and arms and arms and arms and arms and arms and arms and arms. . . .

THE END

You snap off a long, pointed stalagmite. It's a perfect sword! You swing it — and miss both Tiki warriors.

Instead, you slam your weapon into an even bigger stalagmite rising all the way to the ceiling.

"Look out!" Gina shrieks.

The warriors come at you again. Again you swing — and miss.

Hey — so you've got bad aim. You're not a tennis player — you're on the swim team!

Once more, you swing and miss, hitting the huge stalagmite. You hit it so hard, your head spins.

A rumbling sound shakes the cave. Is it thunder? Or is the volcano erupting?

The cave shakes harder. The rumbling gets worse.

"Watch out!" Gina screams. A hunk of the cave ceiling crashes to the ground. Even the two warriors seem terrified.

"Oh, no! The Kalookie Cave is caving in on us!" you shout.

Hurry to PAGE 79.

You toss the eye down to Kala. Immediately, he puts it in the eyehole of the sacred Tiki mask.

Kala holds the mask up for all to see. A third blast of purple vapor explodes. When the smoke clears, you discover the warriors have all disappeared into thin air!

"No!" Hooahtoo screams. "My spirit warriors! They're gone!"

"That's right, Hooahtoo," Kala shouts. "You wanted to use the power of the mask for evil. But I chose to use it for good! The curse is lifted. Thanks for your help, my friends." He smiles up at you. Then he glares at Hooahtoo again. "And now you'll have to deal with some real people — the police!"

Hooahtoo hangs silently from the spear. You almost feel sorry for the little guy.

Almost.

Turn to PAGE 135.

Your eyes widen with horror. You clap your hand over Gina's mouth to muffle her scream. You bite your tongue to keep from screaming yourself.

The tour guide and loudmouthed guy have transformed. Before you stand two Tiki warriors! They carry gleaming spears. Crowns made of dried bones sit on their heads.

"Look at those masks!" Gina gasps.

"Tiki masks," you murmur. "I saw masks like those in a ceremony here last year. But that was just for entertainment. I don't think these two are putting on a show!"

The two masked figures gaze at the flashing sky. They chant words in a language you don't understand. Their tone is low and steady. It sounds like some kind of spell.

You're not sure if they've seen you and Gina. There's a dark hollow underneath a rock next to you. Maybe both of you could fit in there. Should you try to hide? Or should you just stay still?

The lightning flash fades. Darkness saves you. For now.

But you won't be safe for long.

If you try to hide, scurry over to PAGE 90.

If you freeze to avoid attracting their attention, go to PAGE 16.

"Gina!" you shout. You stop and tread water. She spots you and waves. "Gina, come here!" you call again.

"What's wrong?" Gina says, swimming over.

"There's a shark nearby. Let's get into the boat. Quickly!" you reply.

Gina's eyes widen fearfully. Without another word, she swims toward the boat.

By now Kala has started the engine and he races over the reef to pick up you and Gina.

"You're safe!" he cries with relief, helping you into the boat.

The stone is burning your skin! You yank it out of your bathing suit and throw it to the bottom of the boat.

The mysterious eye stares up at you.

Kala glances down. His expression changes from relief to surprise. He bends down to examine the stone.

"No!" he gasps. A look of horror comes over his face.

Go to PAGE 76.

You watch in horrified fascination as ten more skeletons creep out of the thick vegetation. One of them reaches down and pulls Gina up by one arm. She screams, but the skeleton holding her slaps a bony hand over her mouth. Gina twists and turns, trying to free herself. It's hopeless.

The first skeleton snaps his whip again. "Unmask!" he orders.

At once all the skeletons curl their bony fingers around their own necks. You watch in total shock.

The skeletons are pulling off their heads!

You gasp! The skeletons are not skeletons at all. They're men in wet suits designed to look like skeletons.

Unfortunately, the one holding Gina heard you gasp.

"There's her friend!" he cries.

He's spotted you. Now what? You could turn back through the tunnel and try to get help. But they may take Gina, and you'll never find her again.

Or you could try to hide by climbing the tree in front of you.

Whatever you decide, do it NOW!

If you run back through the tunnel, turn to PAGE 23.

If you climb the tree, go to PAGE 104.

"What should I do?" you wail. "Kala said you would tell me."

"Kala is right," Hooahtoo answers slowly. "Listen carefully." He fixes his blind eyes on you. You can't tear your own eyes away.

"You have found a piece of the sacred Tiki mask stolen from the sacred Tiki altar. The eye must be replaced. Then and only then will the curse be lifted from Tiki Island."

You glance at the masks on the wall. None of them is missing an eye. "Where is the Tiki mask?" you ask.

"In the land of fire," Hooahtoo whispers. "In the land of Tiki Magic. That is where the Tiki Eye must go."

Turn to PAGE 122.

You and Gina struggle, but it's no use. You can't escape.

The two warriors shove you and Gina to the floor. Holding their spears at your throats, they order you to lie still. Then they cross to the fire pit at the center of the Kalookie Cave.

The Tiki warriors whisper in a language you don't understand. You shudder as you imagine what they're plotting. Their backs are turned as they busy themselves with something near the fire.

You gaze around the cave. Shadows stretch and shiver across the walls. Spikes of stone that look like upside-down icicles grow out of the floor. Stalagmites. They make you think of gleaming weapons waiting to be seized.

You notice a series of old cave paintings on the walls. They seem to tell a story.

Can they tell you why the Tiki warriors brought you to the Kalookie Cave?

Well, can they? You won't find out here! Get over to PAGE 99!

Dr. Oates stops glaring at you. A smile cracks through his scruffy stubble. "So, it's a lecture you want, eh?" he remarks. "Come with me." Grabbing each of you by an arm, he drags you out of the shack. He marches you toward another, larger hut.

Did Dr. Oates buy your story? you wonder.

"Well, my young friends, it's a lecture you're going to get," Dr. Oates tells you. He gestures for you and Gina to sit. Then he sets a tape recorder on a table. "See you when the lecture is over."

He pushes the start button on the tape player and leaves.

You hear the key turn in the lock.

You and Gina are trapped!

"Welcome to Dr. Oliver Oates's lecture series," the tape begins. "In this five-hour course you will come to understand the development of all of earth's cultures. That's right! Every single one of them! From the most ancient times right to the present. Nothing will be left out. You will learn everything you ever wanted to know. And then some! So sit back, relax, and *enjoy*."

Five hours of lectures? Oh, brother! That's what you get for lying!

Learn your lesson on PAGE 106.

You need that light. Skeletons or no skeletons, you've got to untie Gina. Otherwise it will be impossible for the two of you to escape.

Your fingers fumble nervously as they search for the flashlight. At last you feel the cool metal shaft. You pull the light off your belt and turn it on.

It flickers dimly. You hit it with your palm. Finally, a steady beam gleams. You shine it on Gina.

And scream in horror!

This isn't Gina! It's a skeleton! A fresh one! Shreds of rotting flesh still hang from the bones of whoever this is.

Or was.

A terrible thought enters your mind.

What if this is all that's left of your cousin?

You can't stop screaming!

Turn to PAGE 45.

You decide not to warn the skeleton men of what's about to happen to this lagoon. You grab Gina and run.

The whip-cracking skeleton man notices you. He stops laughing. "They're getting away!" he shouts. He cracks his whip wildly in the air.

You and Gina dash toward the tunnel. Freedom! you think as you run. But just as you're about to enter the tunnel, a hand reaches out from the diamond wall and grabs you.

The hand pulls you up to a row of steel bars. "Save us too!" pleads the woman gripping you. The bars block the entrance to a small cave.

Huddled inside is the group of missing islanders!

Quickly, you glance around.

Aha! There's a lever on the opposite wall.

"This better work," you mutter as you yank the lever down.

It does work! The bars slide open.

"Follow us!" you cry, leading all the prisoners into another tunnel. You glance back once and see the diamond lagoon for the last time.

The noise of the walls tumbling down is the only sound you hear.

Go to PAGE 57.

"Gina?" you call. "Can you hear me?"

No response.

"Gina?" you try again. Your voice echoes in the tunnel.

Then you hear a terrifying sound.

A scream.

Gina's scream!

But where did it come from? Everything echoes in this cave. It's hard to pinpoint the direction of the sound.

You have to find Gina. But where should you look? Did she ever make it into the tunnel? Did she take a different turn and get lost?

Or did the skeleton pirate grab her and drag her back to the ship?

If you go back to the wrecked ship, turn to PAGE 108.

If you stay in the tunnel to look for Gina, turn to PAGE 47.

"Why are you pretending to be pirate skeletons?" you demand.

The whip-cracker snorts. "Why do you think? To scare away nosy tourists like you!"

"What are you going to do to us?" Gina cries.

"It's not what we're going to do *to* you. It's more what you're going to do *for* us," the whip-cracker snarls. "We must get as many of these diamonds out of here as we can before the Kenalua Volcano fires up again. This lagoon is fragile. Even a tremor from Kenalua can upset the ocean floor and cause a cave-in. We've already felt slight movement. Time is running out."

"Even a slight tremor?" you gasp.

"Never mind that now," the whip-cracker snaps. "You can join the others who wandered too far on the reef. We've captured enough of you now to get our work done quickly."

"What?" you exclaim. "So you're the ones who made people disappear! There's no curse on Tiki Island. You're the only curse!"

The whip-cracker and his band of skeleton-suited men laugh. "Yes," says the leader. "I am the curse. And now the curse is on you two!"

Go to PAGE 93.

There's no decision to make here! You're too terrified to look at the ghost, anyway.

Which turns out to be a good thing!

"I remember now!" Dr. Oates cries. "The spirit can't see us as long as we don't look into his eyes. So whatever you do — keep your gaze down!"

"Will he go away?" Gina whispers.

"He's searching for something very important," Dr. Oates explains. "He won't rest until he finds it. It's the only way he can free himself from his ghostly torment."

Dr. Oates glances at you. "I wonder what he would do if he knew that *you* have what he is looking for," he adds softly.

"*I* have it?" you gasp. "You mean the stone piece?"

Dr. Oates nods. "It is the eye he lost in battle. Without it he can never see his way out of his half-living half-dead world."

Something occurs to you. "What were you planning to do with the eye if I gave it to you?" you ask the scruffy archaeologist.

"Put it back where it belongs," Dr. Oates replies. "I wanted to free the Tiki King's spirit. Ever since I read the legend of the Tiki King I've felt sorry for him."

You don't need to hear another word.

You know what you're going to do.

Go to PAGE 39.

"Good idea," you tell Gina. "We can ask Dr. Oates about the stone after we explore. Maybe he'll be calmer by then."

Gina's eyes sparkle with excitement. "Let's see if we can find out what they're digging for," she suggests. "Wouldn't it be cool if we found something ourselves? Like a treasure chest? Or even just an old vase?"

"You can't keep anything you find," you remind her. "The island has a law that artifacts found here belong to the island and have to go to the museum. They want to protect the island's history."

"Oh. Too bad. But it would still be awesome just to find something." Gina gazes around. "Hey, let's check out that shack." She points to a small hut at the edge of the jungle.

You sneak over to the shack. You peek in the window and gasp.

Go to PAGE 85.

"Forget it, bonehead!" you shout.

"Take them below!" Captain Bones orders the crew. "Show no mercy." His jawbone juts out as he thrusts his bony skull close to your face. "You'll talk soon enough," he snarls. "Or you'll never talk again!"

The hatch in the floor of the deck opens. You and Gina are forced down the rickety stairs. You wade through waist-high water.

SLAM! The hatch bangs shut above you. One small torch on the wall casts a yellow glow over the dungeon. "Aaahhhhh!" you scream when you see skeletons hanging in chains from the walls.

"They never got out — and we won't, either!" Gina wails.

Something swims through your legs and back again. "Yikes!" you squeal as the slimy thing brushes against your bare leg.

"What is it?" Gina cries. "I feel it too!"

Whatever it is, it's nibbling at your ankles. You peer down into the water and see schools of vicious-looking fish. Their round spiked heads have huge mouths filled with three rows of razor-sharp teeth.

They surround you!

Go to PAGE 17

There are too many skeletons to fight alone. You have to go for help.

You swim toward the waterfall that dumped you here. The current is against you. Your arms can hardly pull you forward. But you force yourself to continue swimming. I have to get help, you tell yourself over and over. You reach and kick. Reach and kick.

A long, snakelike arm suddenly wraps around you! It pulls you underwater.

You struggle to free yourself, but another arm wraps around you. Then another! And another!

Those aren't arms! They're tentacles! Eight thick tentacles!

Oh, no! You're trapped in the grip of a giant octopus!

Turn to PAGE 133.

"What is that?" Gina asks, staring at the painted stone.

"I don't know," you admit. "But I think Kala does."

"It — it's nothing," Kala stammers. "Just some ocean junk." From his nervous tone, you get the feeling he's lying.

On the ride back to the resort, you notice Kala stealing glances at the stone piece. It seems to make him nervous.

As the boat pulls up to the dock, Kala speaks very softly. "I believe you have found something very important," he tells you. "But you must make sure."

You're glad he's talking to you again. Even if he is acting strange. "But how do I find out what it is?" you ask.

"Go to the village," he tells you, "and find Hooahtoo."

"Who what who?" you repeat.

"Hooahtoo. He will tell you what you have found," Kala explains. "But tell no one about it. And trust no one!"

Gina grabs the snorkeling equipment while you wrap the stone in a towel. Then you and Gina scramble onto the dock. You watch Kala start up the boat and drive away.

"That Kala is one weird dude," Gina comments.

"Maybe . . . ," you reply thoughtfully.

Turn to PAGE 29.

"Okay, okay," you say to Gina. "We'll listen to the guide. But then we have to hurry!"

"Sshhh!" Gina hushes you. "She's talking about the volcano."

"I know you all want to climb to the walkway around the mouth of the volcano," the dark-haired tour guide says.

"Yeah!" a loudmouthed guy calls out from the crowd. "That's why we came all this way!"

"I'm sorry to tell you the tour stops right here," the guide continues. "Kenalua last erupted in nineteen sixty. Before that she erupted in nineteen twenty. Scientists predict her pattern of eruption to be about every forty years. But the growling in Kenalua's belly has been felt recently. Scientists are watching her very closely."

As if on cue, a sudden rumbling sound fills the air.

Turn to PAGE 14.

Too many weird things have happened since you found the Tiki Eye. You have to take Gina's disappearance seriously.

You spend the next few hours searching behind every rock and shrub. You start feeling more and more scared. Kala said people were disappearing. Is Gina one of them now?

You feel the Tiki Eye heating up in your pocket. You take it out for real this time. You throw it as far as you can.

Like a boomerang, the stone piece turns in midair and flies back to you. You catch it and toss it again.

The same thing happens.

No matter how many times you hurl it, the Tiki Eye comes back. But when you try to hold it, the heat burns you.

"Gina!" you cry one last time. "Why can't Gina come back instead of this Tiki Eye? I wish, I wish, I wish I'd never found this dumb thing!"

Turn to PAGE 95.

You realize the stalagmite you banged into was actually a beam holding up the cave's roof. You've loosened it, and now the roof is collapsing. The walls of the cave crack and crumble around you.

You're going to be buried alive. You're all going to be prisoners of the Kalookie Cave.

"I'm sorry!" you cry to Gina.

But Gina can't hear you. Neither can the warriors. They're all smothered under a pile of crumbling rubble. And soon you will be too.

Too bad. But sometimes that's just the way the Kalookie crumbles.

THE END

Your right foot can barely keep up with your left! The Tiki Eye drags you quickly back to the resort.

Along the way, you try to get rid of the eye. You scrape it on a root. You bang your foot against a tree trunk until it hurts.

Nothing works.

The eye sticks to your sneaker as if it were super-glued!

On the dock up ahead you spot Kala's dad, the resort owner. Thank goodness! you think. Maybe he can help. He might know about island curses!

You rush up to the dock. Kala's dad bends down, reaching into a boat tied to the dock.

Oh, no! Before you can call out his name, the eye on your shoe takes control again! You boot Kala's dad right in the behind! He flies off the dock into the water.

"You!" he sputters when his head pops out above the water. "I'm speaking to your mother! You will be banned from all resort activities!"

Your heart sinks. There goes your vacation.

But can you blame him?

No one likes to be kicked in

THE END.

The decision is made. "Okay, let's go see this Hooahtoo guy," you declare.

You and Gina find your way to Hooahtoo's shack in the village.

"Enter," a booming voice calls from inside.

Hey. How did he know you were there? You didn't have time to ring the wind chimes in the doorway yet!

Gina pushes you forward. You nervously pull aside the palm leaves covering the opening. A purple mist hangs in the dark, round room. The sweet smell of mango incense fills the air. Tiki masks cover the walls.

"Show Hooahtoo what you have brought him," the deep voice orders. The speaker is still hidden inside the mist.

This place really gives you the creeps. The smells. The sounds. Everything.

Gina jabs her elbow into your side.

"I . . . my name is . . . ," you stammer.

"Hooahtoo knows who you are," the voice interrupts you. "Hooahtoo knows everything." An arm waves the mist aside.

Gina gasps.

You gulp.

That's Hooahtoo?

Turn to PAGE 19.

A deafening roar bursts from the volcano. A violent tremor knocks you and Gina to the ground.

"Look!" Gina cries. She points to the sky.

Hundreds of ghostly figures rise out of the volcano. And vanish! Wails and cries fill the air. You and Gina lie on the ground, covering your heads with your arms.

Then, as suddenly as it began, all is silent.

You and Gina stare at each other. Slowly, you get to your feet. The ground is steady again. The volcano is quiet.

"The lizard!" Gina cries. "It's gone!"

You dash off the walkway and race to the spot where the lizard had dropped you. You notice a tiny little reptile sunning itself on a rock. "No, Gina," you call. "It's not gone. It's just gone back to its normal size."

So that's it. The curse of Tiki Island has been lifted!

Of course, now that the lizard is only six inches long, it's much harder to ride it home. In fact, when you try to climb on its back, you flatten the poor thing.

Oh, well. It's a happy ending for you and Gina, but for the lizard it's simply

THE END.

Diamonds shower down on you. The walls of the lagoon are caving in. Your shouts were the final blow. Your warning is the very thing that caused these walls to tumble. You watch in horror as the men in skeleton suits are pelted by falling chunks of colored diamonds.

You and Gina try to run for the tunnel, but stumble over the shaking ground. Diamonds, diamonds, and more diamonds rain down. You and Gina are up to your ears in the sparkling jagged-edged jewels. The others are already buried.

You and Gina exchange final glances as the diamond walls continue falling on you. It's over now.

But one thing is for sure, this vacation turned out to be a real gem!

THE END

You square your shoulders and tuck the small box into your pocket. Then you and Gina hurry to the path up the volcano.

As you approach, you see a group of tourists. A tour guide is lecturing about the Kenalua Volcano.

"Let's listen in," Gina suggests, pulling you to a stop.

"We can't," you protest. "Hooahtoo said we have to go *now*."

"Well, I'd kind of like to know what we're getting into," Gina argues.

Gina's got a point. Maybe you should stop and learn more about this volcano.

Then you feel the heat of the stone seeping through the straw box in your pocket.

Do you have time to stop?

If you stop and listen to the guide, turn to PAGE 77.

If you keep going, turn to PAGE 130.

"Gina! Look! This place is full of treasure!" You gaze through the dirty window at pots, spears, and vases lining the walls. "And look at all those masks! I think they're real Tiki masks!"

"What are Tiki masks?" Gina asks.

Kala told you all about Tiki masks last year. "They're masks that island warriors used to wear for celebrations and dances," you explain.

You sneak inside the shack to get a closer look. Pieces of clay pottery and even whole pots are set out and labeled. On a large table beads, necklaces, rings, and gold pieces covered with dirt wait for sorting.

You notice a stack of cartons piled in a corner. As you examine them, you realize these boxes are the *real* find.

Each carton is packed and sealed. And they're all addressed to The Ancient Artifacts Emporium in New York City!

"Check this out," you call to Gina.

"Hey!" Gina exclaims, staring at the cartons. "I thought you said nothing could leave the island."

"They can't," you reply. "But I guess Dr. Oates doesn't —"

A booming voice interrupts you. "Did someone mention my name?" A scruffy-faced man leans through the open window.

It's Dr. Oates!

Go to PAGE 125.

With a shout, Kala leads the charge of prisoners. As they storm down the aisles, Hooahtoo stands on his throne.

"You will obey the great Hooahtoo!" he shrieks. "I am the supreme leader! I will rule Tiki Island! Obey! Obey! Obey!"

The freed islanders herd the Tiki warriors into the prison. The steel bars crash down.

Next, Kala's army surrounds Hooahtoo. They hoist him high into the air. Kala grabs a Tiki spear and pins him to the cave wall.

Hanging by his purple robe, the tiny madman can do no more harm.

When it's all over, Kala glances up to the ledge where you and Gina perch. He waves and smiles just the way he used to. You grin and wave back. You're glad he's back to his normal self.

You glance down and see the Tiki Eye lying near your feet. It must have slipped out of your pocket.

You hold it for the last time. It's warm in your hand.

"Here, Kala!" you call. "Catch!"

Go to PAGE 61.

You're standing face-to-face with an army of Tiki warriors!

Not just Tiki warriors — Tiki warrior *spirits*!

Each one of the masks from the mask room is now worn by a ghostly warrior. There are *hundreds* of spirits. And they're angry!

"We've been held prisoner long enough!" one wails.

"The door!" moans another. "It's open! It's finally open!"

The warrior spirits rush through the door, nearly trampling you and Gina. There are so many of them, they fill the cave.

What will they do to you and Gina?

You don't have to wait long for your answer. They crowd around you. You feel yourself being lifted high into the air. Gina is held aloft also.

"They have rescued us!" a warrior shouts.

"Our new leaders!" another adds.

The warriors carry you on their shoulders. You're scared at first. But then you decide it's kind of nice to be a leader.

The only problem: What is your mom going to say when you get back to the hotel? Because the room is sure going to be crowded now!

THE END

"The eye!" you whisper. "It's our only hope!"

Gina nods. "Do it!" she urges.

You reach into your pocket and pull out . . . a quarter!

You grope around in your pocket.

All you come up with is lint.

"It's gone!" you gasp. "I must have dropped it!"

"Now what will we do?" Gina cries. "Hooahtoo says two must die! I have a feeling I know which two he means!"

Maybe you want to rethink that last choice.

Throwing a rock might be a very good idea right about now!

Go to PAGE 15.

You decide you don't trust this guy. There's no way you're going to tell him about your mysterious piece of stone.

For all you know, he'll pack it up and sell it to a collector in New York!

"We didn't mean to trespass," you declare. "We saw your sign in the village and we came to hear your lecture. Education is really, really important. I mean, I think everybody should go to school. Otherwise there would be kids running all over the place. In the mall. On the street. Know what I mean?"

You know you're babbling, but you can't seem to stop.

"Yes?" Dr. Oates snaps. "And what is the point of all this nonsense?"

"Well, and, so we were just looking for the um . . . ah . . ."

"Lecture hall!" Gina fills in for you.

Go to PAGE 67.

You and Gina take advantage of the darkness and crowd into the dark hollow under the rock.

Whoops! It's not a hollow.

It's a hole.

Instantly you feel a suction pulling you down. Sour-smelling juices well up around you. The juices wash back and forth against your skin until it feels raw.

How could you possibly know the hole was really the open mouth of a hungry Lava Lizard? You're in the giant lizard's stomach — and his digestive juices are already at work digesting you!

Ever since the Kenalua Volcano erupted years ago, the mountain has been alive with these lizards. They're the color of the lava rock and blend in with the rocky lava cliffs. No one ever sees them. Until it's too late. This is a tough way to end your vacation, but look at the bright side. . . .

Oh, never mind. There is no bright side. Everything is dark inside a Lava Lizard's gut.

THE END

You grab the broken stone piece and head for the door. Before you can shove aside the wide palm leaf, something burns your hand.

"Ouch!" you shout. Your flesh sizzles! The stone piece is frying your skin!

You drop it to the ground.

You halt at the doorway, clutching your burned hand.

Gina stops behind you. "What's wrong?" she asks.

You hold out your hand to show her. You're in too much pain to speak.

"Whoa!" Gina gasps. She gazes at your palm. "It's the eye!"

Smoke rises from the center of your palm. As it wafts away, the outline of an eye is revealed.

It's burned like a tattoo into your hand.

Hooahtoo laughs. "You cannot take it. You cannot leave it. The curse is upon you now."

Go to PAGE 65.

You hold your hand out again toward the lizard. "Take us where we need to go!" you instruct the creature.

Gina stares at you. "Do you honestly believe that's going to work?" she demands.

You shrug. "Do you have a better idea?" you challenge her.

"Well, no," she admits. "I guess it's worth a shot."

Strangely, the lizard seems to understand. It rolls back over to allow you and Gina to climb onto its back. Then, with a huge grunt, the reptile lifts itself off the ground. It stomps out of the mask room and back into the dark tunnel.

"Where do you think it will take us?" Gina asks.

"I don't know," you say. "But I'm hoping it will at least get us away from the Tiki warriors."

It's hard to stay on the slippery scaly skin. You and Gina cling as well as you can to the beast's back. After a while you realize the lizard has been steadily going uphill. You begin to tremble.

You know where you're headed.

Go to PAGE 22.

The whip-cracking skeleton man throws his head back and laughs. Big, deep belly laughs. All of the fake skeltons laugh now, louder and louder. Their evil laughter echoes through the diamond lagoon, bouncing from one sparkling wall to another. The noise is so loud, it could cause an avalanche!

RUMBLE!

Uh-oh. What's that? Is it your imagination, or is the lagoon really trembling under your feet?

RUMBLE! RUMBLE!

No. It's not your imagination at all!

Should you warn the skeleton men to stop laughing before it's too late? Or should you let nature take its course and try to escape when the walls of the lagoon tumble?

If you warn the laughing skeleton men, go to PAGE 44.

If you let the walls come tumbling down, go to PAGE 69.

You rush over to Gina, ready to yank the mask off her face.

"Just kidding!" Gina crows. She pulls off the purple Tiki mask easily and drops it on the pile of the other rejected masks. "Got you!" she teases.

"You jerk!" you scold. But you can't help chuckling. You and Gina burst out laughing.

Then you notice the masks on the wall trembling slightly. *"Shhh!"* you hush Gina. She stops giggling immediately.

You and Gina stare at the masks on the wall. They *click* and *clack* as some unseen force shakes the room. You hear pounding.

Footsteps!

Huge, heavy, loud footsteps!

"Wh-wh-what's that?" Gina stammers.

"Whatever it is," you murmur, "it's big!"

You glance around, searching for a way out. There's a tunnel on the other side of the room. But that's where the footsteps are coming from!

The only other way out is the way you came in — through the secret door. Which leads back into the cave with the waiting Tiki warriors!

The footsteps are even louder now! What should you do?

If you take your chances with the Tiki warriors and run back through the secret door, turn to PAGE 18.

If you think you'll have better luck staying where you are, turn to PAGE 105.

As soon as you make the wish, everything changes! You're no longer standing on the volcano searching for Gina. You're back in the water, snorkeling!

Brightly colored fish dart through the purple coral. To your surprise, Gina taps you on the shoulder. She points to an opening in the reef. It's an undersea cave. She wants you to explore it with her.

You're about to follow Gina. You glance down at the ocean floor. You thought you saw something gleaming.

But there's nothing there. No, you realize, I must have been seeing things.

Then you pop your head out of the water. You notice Kala waving and yelling from the boat. A shadow slices through the water. Now you remember.

It's a shark!

Go to PAGE 52.

"Why should they be afraid of an old mask?" Gina demands.

"*Ssshhh!*" you whisper. You yank Gina behind a bush to watch.

Oates strides out of the shack. Every worker he passes falls to the ground. Some scream in fear. Some kneel before Oates as if he were royalty.

"Don't you see?" you murmur to Gina. "There must be a power connected with the Tiki mask. Wearing it makes him a leader of some kind. That's why he wanted the mask so badly."

Gina gasps. "Look!" She points a shaky finger toward the opposite edge of the jungle.

Your body trembles. Dozens of figures wearing Tiki masks creep out of the jungle!

Turn to PAGE 131.

Dr. Oates sure is moody, you think. He swings from nice to mean to nice awfully fast.

So fast that he's already back to smiling.

"I must have that Tiki Eye," he tells you. "I'll give you money for it. I'm willing to pay any amount. Within reason, of course."

You glance at Gina. You can see she's thinking what you're thinking. Some extra cash could come in very handy while you're on vacation.

"Well," you begin. "Would fifty dollars be fair?"

Dr. Oates laughs. "Fifty dollars! No, that's not fair. I'll give you each one hundred dollars! Now *that's* fair!"

Is it?

You wonder what makes this broken stone piece worth anything at all.

If you take the money, turn to PAGE 30.
If you turn down the offer, turn to PAGE 13.

"Swim, Gina!" you shout. "Swim away!"

You and Gina desperately stroke through the water. You glance back over your shoulder. You watch in horror as the skeleton leaps off the ragged-edged deck and glides effortlessly toward you.

"He's after us!" you scream. How can a skeleton swim? you wonder. His dried, white bones rattle against each other as he races to catch up with you.

You and Gina swim as fast as you can. But the terrifying bone man is gaining. A wide-brimmed, feathered pirate hat casts a shadow over his skeleton face. But you can see his mouth wide open in an angry scream.

When you reach the black sand shore, he's right behind you. Breathlessly, you tear off your snorkeling gear and toss it on the beach. Gina is right behind you. You notice several tunnels in the wall of the cave. You dart into the nearest one.

"Follow me, Gina!" you yell. Your legs are unstoppable now. You race into the tunnel, leading the way. Your heart pounds as you dash through the twists and turns. Then you glance behind you.

Both Gina and the skeleton are gone!

Turn to PAGE 70.

In the first painting, four figures gather around a fire in a cave. Two of the figures are Tiki warriors. Two are kids dressed in shorts and T-shirts.

Like you and Gina.

In the next panel, the warriors hold long-handled tools over the fire. Each tool ends in a different shape. One has a sun. The other has a moon.

You gasp when you see the third panel! In it, the Tiki warriors are using the tools to brand the kids!

A movement near the fire distracts you from the terrifying wall paintings. The two Tiki warriors turn around. And they're holding red-hot branding tools!

Just like the ones in the paintings on the wall!

Things are getting too hot to handle!

"Flash the Tiki Eye at them," Gina urges.

You don't know what the Tiki Eye's powers might be. Maybe it will scare them off. Or maybe it will just make them angry.

You glance at the sharp stalagmites rising from the cave floor. Could you use one as a weapon?

Do something! Unless you want to smell burning flesh! *Yours!*

If you flash the Tiki Eye at the warriors, turn to PAGE 33.

If you grab a stalagmite and use it as a sword, turn to PAGE 60.

That's because he *has* seen a ghost!

A second later, you and Gina see the ghost too.

A twelve-foot-tall mass of vapor takes shape. A scarred and scratched Tiki mask appears where the head should be. War paint decorates its shimmering arms and legs.

"Oh, no!" Dr. Oates murmurs. "It's the spirit of the Tiki King. There are many legends about him. He died trying to take over the island. He failed. Now he walks as a ghost, still attempting to win his last battle."

"Do the legends say if he's dangerous?" you ask nervously.

"V-v-very dangerous," Dr. Oates stammers.

"Do the legends tell how to escape?" Gina is so frightened, her voice squeaks.

Dr. Oates anxiously rubs his face. "I-I-I can't remember!" he cries.

The ghost seems to be searching for something. Trees topple as he yanks them out of the ground. Dirt and stones fly as the spirit kicks aside bushes and plants.

And now, he's headed straight toward you!

Keep your knees from shaking until PAGE 37.

"No!" you cry. "Don't throw us in the brig. We'll lead you out of here. We'll do anything you say. Just let us go. Please!"

"A wise decision," Captain Bones snaps. Then he turns to the skeleton crew. "Bring the treasure!" he commands.

The skeletons hurriedly lift trunk after trunk filled with gold, gems, and jewels they stole from the Tiki Islanders years ago. "Lead the way, then," Captain Bones orders you. "And don't try any funny business!"

You and Gina dive over the side of the pirate ship. The skeleton crew jumps in after you. Even with the weight of the treasure chests they manage to swim through the water.

"What will we do now?" Gina whispers as she swims next to you. "Are we really going to let them go through with their plan to take over Tiki Island?"

"Not if my own plan works," you reply. "Go along with what I say and do."

Go to PAGE 127.

"Get it off of me!" you yell. You shake your foot as hard as you can. The eye doesn't budge. It stares up at you.

Your heart pounds as you realize the truth. "Hooahtoo was right," you wail. "It's the curse! The eye will be on me wherever I go!"

"Just kick it off," Gina orders.

"Don't you think I'm trying?" you snap. You shake your foot again. The stone fragment doesn't move.

Gina kneels down. She tries to pry the stone eye from your sneaker.

Without warning, your foot suddenly kicks out. It knocks Gina hard on the chin. She flies backwards several feet.

"Gina!" you cry. "I'm sorry! I didn't mean to —"

Gina cuts you off. "Forget it!" she huffs. "That's no way to treat someone who's trying to help!" She storms away.

You gaze after her sadly. She'll never believe that it was the Tiki Eye on your shoe that made you kick her. It was as if it was controlling your foot!

And now, the eye on your sneaker is making you walk!

Fast!

Quick! Race-walk to PAGE 80.

The dirt walls are covered with masks. "There are even more masks than there are lizards!" you exclaim. "There must be a zillion Tiki masks in here!"

"This must be where the special Tiki mask is hidden!" Gina declares. She stares at the enormous collection of masks. "But how will we ever figure out which mask is the right one?"

"It's obvious!" you exclaim. "The correct mask is the one that's missing an eye, dummy!"

Gina glares at you. "Well, duhhh," she says, rolling her eyes. "Who are you calling dummy, dummy?"

She waves a hand at the collection of masks.

You step closer to the wall, to take a better look.

"Oh," you murmur.

Sigh in frustration. Then turn to PAGE 117.

104

You try to pull yourself up the smooth tree trunk. But you've barely moved an inch when two of the unmasked men in skeleton wet suits run and grab you. They drag you down and throw you next to Gina.

"You found me!" Gina exclaims.

"You may regret it," the fake skeleton with the whip grunts. "Okay, you nosy kids," he continues. "So you two wanted to do some exploring, eh? You should have quit when you found the shipwreck. You should have settled for a few crummy gold coins and gone back to where you came from. You don't really think we're going to share the diamonds with you, do you?"

"We didn't even know the diamonds were here," you sputter. "We don't want them. We just want to get back to the Tiki Resort."

"Ha!" the man with the whip laughs. He snaps his whip in the air and brings his face next to yours. "Sorry, kid," he says. "There's no going back. Your exploring days are over!"

Go to PAGE 71.

You don't want to risk opening the door. You don't want to face those Tiki warriors again.

Boom! Boom! Boom! Boom! The pounding footsteps come closer.

Closer. Closer.

Your mouth opens to scream. But you are too terrified to make a sound.

Then the largest lizard you've ever seen emerges from the tunnel and enters the mask room. It's so huge, its back brushes against the ceiling. Its flicking tongue reaches nearly across the room.

It takes another heavy step toward you. The Tiki masks rattle and fall to the floor. The lizard flicks its split tongue at you, missing you by inches. Gina collapses to the floor beside you.

The monstrous reptile takes another step closer. Again, it flicks out its tongue. Now you can see the rows of sharp teeth gleaming in its gigantic mouth.

"Eyyyyahhh!" you shriek. You hold up your hands to protect your face.

The lizard lifts its huge webbed foot.

And freezes.

Go to PAGE 58.

You don't know how you stand it, but finally the five-hour course ends.

The tape finishes.

Gina snores in the corner. You stand and stretch. Then Dr. Oates unlocks the door and enters smiling.

"So?" he asks. "Did you enjoy my lectures?"

"Well, um . . . ," you stammer, not sure of what to say.

But it doesn't matter. Before you can respond, Dr. Oates grips your arm. He brings his face close to yours. "Now tell me why you're *really* here," he demands.

You have no choice. You unroll your towel to show Dr. Oates the stone piece.

But it's not there!

It's disappeared!

Turn to PAGE 28. Maybe the mysterious eye is over there, looking around!

"Gina!" you scream. But she can't hear you over the roar of the churning lava pool below. You don't know what you want to say, anyway. Maybe just "good-bye."

You're about to yell your farewell. You clear your throat.

Then you remember the Tiki Eye. It saved you before.

Maybe it can save you again.

You face the eye toward the ocean of liquid fire. The glow of the eye meets the glow of the hot lava. For a second, nothing happens.

Than a powerful jet of hot wind whooshes up from below. It blows you and Gina upward. Higher and higher. Farther and farther from the fire.

You hold the Tiki Eye to your lips and kiss it. "Thank you!" you shout.

The wind changes direction. With the power of a tornado, you and Gina fly into a small chamber inside the volcano mountain. You hit the rock wall with a *THUD!* and fall to the ground.

Turn to PAGE 34.

108

The skeleton must have grabbed Gina. You turn around and race back out of the tunnel. You stand on the shore, gazing at the shipwreck in the blue-black water.

You gasp! The horrible skeleton is dragging Gina through a window in the side of the ship!

You dive into the pool and swim toward the tilting ship. "I'm coming, Gina," you whisper to yourself. "Don't worry!"

You swim underwater most of the way. As you approach the half-sunken ship, you open your eyes underwater to see it. The pink glow from the cave walls lights the scene.

The ship is huge! Its hull is stabbed by the rotted half hull of another ship. Treasure is scattered about the ocean floor like so much ocean junk. Gold coins, pearls, rubies, emeralds, and sapphires dot the sand.

You'd love to take a closer look. Exploring a pirate ship filled with treasure would be awesome! But Gina needs you on deck.

Besides, two very scary-looking skeletons stand guard inside the ripped hull of the ship.

Turn to PAGE 32.

"Come on, Gina," you say hurriedly. "Follow that guy!" You start up the mountain.

"But the volcano!" Gina gasps, scrambling after you.

"Hooahtoo said we're in danger as long as we have the stone piece," you remind Gina. "He also told us we have to go to the volcano to get rid of it. The volcano erupting may be the danger he was talking about."

"Just throw it away!" Gina pleads. She stops climbing. "Let someone else find it and put it back. Besides, you're at the foot of the volcano. Maybe this is close enough!"

Gina's face is red, and she's almost shouting.

You don't want her to be mad at you. And maybe she's right. The volcano could be dangerous.

But if you throw the stone away down here, will the curse go away with it?

Or will the curse be worse because you didn't follow Hooahtoo's instructions?

Maybe you should *pretend* to throw the stone away. Later, when Gina is calmer, you can continue your mission.

If you throw the stone piece up the mountain, turn to PAGE 124.

If you pretend to throw it away to calm Gina, turn to PAGE 24.

110

"We didn't *give* it to him, he bought it!" Gina protests. "We have to get out of here! What if he looks at *us* through those evil Tiki Eyes? Please! Let's go!"

"All right," you agree. "Let's go!"

You dart down the path. But a figure in a Tiki mask blocks your way. You turn around and face another silent Tiki guard. You're surrounded. And so is Gina!

You know Gina is surrounded, because you can see her *through* the Tiki guard in front of you.

Gulp!

That's right.

You can see through all of the Tiki guards.

These aren't Dr. Oates's masked workers. These are full-fledged Tiki warrior spirits. Commanded by the wearer of the Tiki mask. And you-know-who is in charge!

Dr. Oates bellows more of the terrible chant:

"Tiki Eye! Tiki Eye!
Use your power
Make them —"

Well, you know the rest. No need to rub it in. Why torture you with the awful words? Let's just get this over with.

But don't feel too bad. You were very brave. Right up to

THE END.

You take the deepest breath you can. Then you swim after Gina toward the cave in the reef. You know the shark is close behind. You hope the cave entrance will be too small for the huge fish.

You squeeze through the opening. You don't dare glance back at the shark. You just keep following behind Gina, swimming deeper into the cave.

This is deeper than you've ever snorkeled before. The cave darkens as the walls come closer and closer together. It's more like an underwater tunnel than a cave. You worry that soon you won't be able to fit through. What if you get stuck in here?

Your lungs start to ache. You'll need to come up for air soon. The shark *must* have given up by now, you think.

But before you can motion to Gina to turn around, a strong current sucks you farther into the cave. And deeper underwater!

Your lungs are going to explode if you don't breathe soon!

Go to PAGE 6.

You swim around to the other side of the creaking ship. Wrapping your fingers over the railing, you pull yourself onto the deck. You hide behind a stack of barrels.

Several groups of skeletons in torn pirate clothes are talking on the deck. Some growl angrily about the captain who brought them to this watery grave. Others say they plan to take their riches and walk among the living again.

But it's the group at the far end, the one in the shadows, that grabs your attention! They have Gina! And they're shoving her into a tiny closet.

"She'll keep here until she's bones like us!" a skeleton snarls. You shudder when you notice one side of his skull is missing.

"Aye!" shouts a short skeleton with one arm. "Now that she's seen us, she cannot leave the cave. And once we find the other child, our treasure is safe again!"

Go to PAGE 25.

"Evil?" Kala shouts. He sits up, his eyes flashing angrily. "I am not the evil here! It is you! And you! And you!"

He points a shaking finger at you, and Gina, and Dr. Oates. "Tourists! Archaeologists! Destroyers! You want to take Tiki Island from us. Tiki Island shall belong to me. I will save it from all of you!"

"But Kala," you say. "I'm your friend. We ..."

But Kala interrupts you. It seems as if he's gone crazy. "A few months ago I saw the sacred mask in a dream. A voice told me I had a mission: Find the missing eye! Save the island! I heard the voices of the Tiki warrior spirits commanding me!"

You watch horrified as Kala paces around the tent. Could the other Tiki Eye have put a kind of spell on him? you wonder. Seeing him now, you think it could be possible.

"But now I have it! And I shall rule!" Kala bends over and picks up a piece of the shattered mask. He turns it toward you and Gina and Dr. Oates.

It's the Tiki Eye!

Turn to PAGE 132.

You have to do something. But what?

"The Tiki mask!" you cry. "We have to take it away from him!"

"But how can we do that when he's wearing it?" Gina asks.

"I haven't figured out that part yet," you admit. You watch Dr. Oates stroll through the masked workers and warriors. They all seem to be hypnotized by him.

"I have an idea," you whisper. "Follow me."

You lead Gina to the shack where you discovered the cartons. You sneak in through the back window. "Keep your eye on Dr. Oates," you instruct Gina. "Tell me if he heads this way."

Gina positions herself by the window. You tear open a box and rummage through it.

"What are you looking for?" Gina asks.

"This!" you announce. "And this!" You pull two Tiki masks out of the box. They look like the masks the workers wear. "Here." You hand one to Gina. "Put this on. Dr. Oates won't recognize us in these. Maybe we'll be able to get close enough to steal back the mask."

"If he doesn't put a spell on us first," Gina remarks grimly.

Go to PAGE 136.

"Get up!" you hear a man's voice order.

Where is he? Who is he talking to? you wonder. You duck behind one of the exotic trees. Has he seen you?

You gaze across the lagoon. There he is! You see a large man in a tattered uniform. His back is to you. He stands over someone lying on the ground.

Gina!

He's talking to Gina! The man cracks his whip in the air above her head. Gina covers her face with her arms and huddles on the ground.

You have to help her! Your legs shake with fear, but you manage to stand. They still haven't seen you. You crouch behind the thick tree trunk. You try to figure out what to do.

Then the whip cracker turns around.

You grab hold of the tree to steady yourself.

He's the skeleton you saw on the shipwreck!

Go to PAGE 64.

116

"Tiki Eye!" Hooahtoo bellows, turning in your direction. "Tiki Eye!"

The warriors stand silent. Only Hooahtoo's evil-sounding voice echoes through the cavern. "Tiki Eye sees us!" He slowly spits out each word. "We do not see Tiki Eye!"

He gazes around the cavern. His blind white eyes glisten.

He fixes his unblinking stare on the spot where you peer over the edge. Then he speaks his most terrifying words: "Tiki Eye says two must die!"

"He knows we're up here!" you gasp.

Hooahtoo points a long, bony finger at you and Gina. "Seize them!" he commands. "Bring them to me!"

If you think holding up the Tiki Eye might save you again, turn to PAGE 88.

If you throw a rock at Hooahtoo, turn to PAGE 15.

Every single mask is missing an eye!

The mask task seems impossible. But you don't have a choice. You hold the stone eye up to mask after mask, searching for a match. After a few minutes, you and Gina have tried at least fifty of them.

With no luck.

"That one looks pretty important." Gina points to a dark purple mask with feathers around the edge. Its one eye is wide open and rimmed with purple.

"Okay," you say. "We'll try it." You lift the mask down and place the stone piece over the empty eyehole. "Another dud," you announce. "The stone eye is huge compared to the hole."

You hand the mask to Gina and reach for another one. Gina puts on the mask and growls, "*Aarrrgh!* Do I scare you?"

"Yeah. As if." You snort. "It's just a mask."

"Maybe it's a haunted mask," Gina suggests. She giggles. "Like the one in the GOOSEBUMPS book. Remember? The girl puts the scary mask on and then can't take it off?"

"Yeah, I remember," you reply, "but this isn't anything like that mask. Now take it off. We have a lot more masks to try!"

Gina tugs on the purple mask. "Uhn!" she grunts. "That's weird. I can't seem to get it off. It's stuck!"

Turn to PAGE 94.

118

"The kid's right!" a one-legged pirate skeleton hisses. "The Captain will try to cheat us!"

"Are you sure the treasure is still all here?" Gina asks.

"I'd count it all if I were you," you suggest.

Three skeletons lift a trunk into the air. Then they dump the contents onto the black sand.

"Hey!" Captain Bones bellows. "What are you doing?"

"It's what *you're* doing that worries us!" snaps the one-legged pirate.

Now all the other skeletons are arguing. Some shove gems into their pockets. Others count gold coins. Skeletons begin pushing and shoving, trying to keep the treasure for themselves.

"Mutiny!" Captain Bones cries. "This is mutiny!"

The skeletons pull swords! They attack each other!

"Now!" you whisper to Gina.

Grabbing a treasure chest, you and Gina race to the stairs. You start climbing the slippery rock steps. Kelp and sea moss cover the stone, making it very hard to keep your footing.

Go to PAGE 46.

Tiki Island — doomed? "This is terrible!" you whisper.

The closet door flies open. A skeleton steps forward and yanks you and Gina out. You both tremble so much, you can hardly stand.

"Give the order, Captain Bones!" the crowd of skeletons shouts.

The skeleton called Captain Bones bares his yellowed teeth and hisses at you. "Tiki Island belongs to us. We fought for it. We died for it. Those who died, should live. Those who live, should die! The island and all this treasure belong to us. We stole it fair and square!"

He points to trunks of treasure piled on the deck. The skeleton crew has packed it all up to transport above ground. They're waiting for you to show them the way.

You're too terrified to speak. Captain Bones cackles and leans his bony head into your face. "Not ready to talk yet, eh?" he snarls. "Well, we've got all the time in the world. And all the time in the next world too!"

Go to PAGE 56.

Gina falls to the ground, holding her stomach and laughing. You fluff up your beard. "Hooahtoo orders this volcano to awaken."

Your Hooahtoo act makes you and Gina hysterical. You flop down beside Gina, snorting and giggling.

A sudden explosion at the top of the volcano startles you both into silence. A shower of hot gravel pours down from the top of the mountain. Violent rumbling shakes you, Gina, and everything else on the mountain.

"Oh, no!" Gina cries. "Look what you've done!"

"Did I do that?" you gasp. "The volcano really *is* erupting!"

"Hold on to something!" Gina shouts.

You clutch at shrubs and roots. But everything you grab is ripped from your hands. The earth slides down the rumbling mountain.

"Help!" Gina screams. "I'm falling!" She tumbles past you in a rock slide.

You reach out and grab Gina's foot to try to stop her from sliding away. Instead of pulling her up to you, she drags you down with her!

Tumble to PAGE 55.

Take a look at the tangle of octopus arms below. See that little dot at the bottom of one of the arms? Know what that is? It's you!

Yes, you.

And there's only one way out.

Do it for Gina! She needs you!

Turn to PAGE 59

Start here

Turn to PAGE 11

"Here," you say, pushing the stone piece toward Hooahtoo with your foot. "Take it. You return the Tiki Eye. We didn't come on this vacation to open a repair shop for broken Tiki masks!"

"No, my friend," Hooahtoo replies solemnly. "It is you who found the piece. It is you who must replace it. Nothing will be the same until the Tiki Mask is restored."

"Oh, all right," you grumble. This guy is probably too small to lift the stone eye, anyway. "Just tell us where the mask is, and we'll put back the missing piece."

Hooahtoo nods. "You must climb the highest mountain on Tiki Island. You must pass through the wall of Tiki warriors. Only then will you lift the curse from Tiki Island."

You feel the color drain from your face. "But the highest mountain on Tiki Island is Kenalua," you stammer.

"I've heard of Kenalua," Gina says. "Isn't that the famous —"

"Volcano," you finish for her. "And it's active!"

Turn to PAGE 49.

Finally Dr. Oates strides over to the tent. Just as he steps across the threshold, you and Gina yank the vine! Oates trips over it and sprawls flat on his face.

The Tiki mask flies off. It crashes to the ground, shattering in a thousand pieces!

Before Dr. Oates can get up, you and Gina pounce on his back. Together you pin him on the floor.

"No!" Dr. Oates cries. "No! You've destroyed the mask! You've destroyed me!"

Just then you hear a muffled cry coming from a trunk in the corner of the tent. "Hold him down, Gina!" you instruct her. "He must have locked someone in that trunk!"

You run to the trunk and throw open the top. When you see who's inside, you do a double take.

"Dr. Oates!" you exclaim. "What are *you* doing in there?"

Go to PAGE 35.

124

You decide Gina is right. You'll throw the Tiki Eye up the mountain and forget about it.

You hurl the broken stone piece as hard as you can. As soon as the eye leaves your hand, the rumbling of the volcano grows louder. The earth beneath your feet shakes violently.

"She's gonna blow!" the loudmouthed tourist yells. He grabs a tree and holds on.

"It's the curse!" you cry. "I shouldn't have thrown away the eye. I have to get it back!"

You scramble across the trembling ground. Gina follows you up the mountain. You frantically search the area where the stone piece might have landed.

The whole mountain shakes. The loudmouthed guy stumbles and falls. He tumbles past you and Gina. The tour guide tries to grab him. But he knocks her over, dragging her along with him.

"Gina!" you cry. "Hold on to me!" But before Gina can grab you, the top of the mountain explodes! Hot lava spills down the side of the mountain.

You and Gina are right in the path of the fiery liquid.

Turn to PAGE 8.

"Oh . . . ," you stammer. "We were just . . ."

"You see, we wanted to . . . ," Gina sputters.

"You were just snooping around and you wanted to poke your noses where they don't belong. Is that what you're trying to say?" Dr. Oates bellows.

Before you can answer, he ducks his head back out the window. A second later, he storms through the door. His gray eyes flash. He plants his hands on his hips. "Did you ever hear of trespassing?" he snarls.

"Yes, but we didn't mean to . . ." you begin. You're so upset, you're not sure what to say.

Should you even mention the bit of stone that's in your pocket? Should you tell him the truth about why you came? Or should you just make up something and get out quickly?

If you tell him the truth, and nothing but the truth, turn to PAGE 51.

If you lie like a rug, turn to PAGE 89.

Your eyes land on the cave paintings. Now you can see the final panel. It shows the two kids in T-shirts and shorts sneaking through a secret door in the rock wall!

You yank Gina into the protective glow of the Tiki Eye.

"We have to find that secret door," you murmur to Gina. You point to the wall painting.

"But it doesn't show where the door is!" Gina complains.

"Well, it's here somewhere," you insist.

The Tiki warriors glare at you. But as long as you hold the glowing Tiki Eye, you're safe.

You notice the cave wall is smoother near the last panel of the painting. "I have an idea," you whisper. "Stay close."

Holding the Tiki Eye toward the warriors, you and Gina scurry across the cave. But instead of one door, you find two!

"Which one?" Gina cries.

"I don't know," you admit. You examine the doors closely. There are no knobs. Just a hand-print carved into each door.

"Maybe . . . ," you murmur. You have a feeling that the handprints are the way in. One door has a right handprint, the other a left handprint. There's only one way to decide!

If you are right-handed, turn to PAGE 12.
If you are left-handed, turn to PAGE 50.

You reach the waterfall that swept you and Gina to the pirate ship. You point to the stone staircase carved into the cave wall. "That's the way out, Captain Bones," you announce. "But we should wait until everyone is ashore with the treasure before we climb up."

As the skeletons drag the treasure chests onto the black sand at the base of the stairs, you and Gina wander among them.

"So, how much of the treasure do you think Ol' Bony is going to let you keep?" you ask a pair of grinning skeletons.

"Why, our share!" the taller one declares.

You raise your voice a bit so more of the skeleton crew can hear you. "And how is your share decided? By rank? By how hard you worked to get it?"

The skeletons begin grumbling and murmuring.

"Won't Captain Bones try to keep it all for himself?" Gina adds. She winks at you. She's figured out your plan.

When you snuck aboard you overheard a group of skeletons complaining. This group doesn't strike you as a very loyal bunch. It should be easy to stir up trouble!

It is!

Turn to PAGE 118.

The second he sees you, Kala jumps into the water. He helps you and Gina drag the treasure chest to the boat. You scramble aboard.

Kala's father is the first to realize what the chest holds. "It's the lost treasure of Tiki Island!" he exclaims happily. "The markings on the chest are of the old Tiki tribe robbed by pirates long ago."

Kala and his father go back later for the rest of the treasure. But the passageway is blocked. That's okay, you figure. At least the skeleton pirates can't get out!

All is as it should be on Tiki Island. The people are friendly again. The curse has been lifted. Tourists will soon return. You and Gina are heroes. You're even given a bit of treasure as a reward.

"So what do you say, Gina?" you ask. "Want to go snorkeling?"

"I've had enough excitement for one day," she says. "How about a nice walk on Mount Kenalua instead?"

"But that's a volcano!" you tell her.

She shrugs. "After the adventure we've had, even a volcano would seem nice and calm."

You laugh. But you can't help but wonder if this is truly

THE END.

You call Gina one more time. She doesn't answer.

"That's it," you mutter. You're going to teach her a lesson. Instead of looking for her anymore, you're going to hide and pop out when she walks by.

You duck behind a huge boulder jutting out from the side of the mountain. When you lean against the boulder, it moves! As it rolls forward, you lose your balance. The next thing you know, you're falling into a deep hole.

"Gina-a-a-a-a-a-a-a-a!" you cry as you tumble down through darkness.

Land on PAGE 34.

You have to keep going. The stone is burning a hole in your pocket. And while these tourists are listening to the guide, you and Gina can get a head start up the mountain.

Along the way you discover tufts of cottony white fluff popping out of pod plants. "This stuff is cool," you exclaim. "It looks like popcorn!"

You grab a handful. You toss it at Gina. It lands in her hair. "Cut it out," she complains. She brushes the white fluff away with a giggle. "Hey — it's like dry snowballs!"

You snatch up more of the white stuff. When you collect enough, you'll dump it on Gina. You can have a fluff fight!

Soon your arms are full of the stuff. It piles up past your chin. Gina glances at you and starts laughing.

"What's so funny?" you demand.

"The fluff! It gives you a white beard!" She giggles again. "It makes you look like Hooahtoo!"

"Oh, yeah!" You laugh too. "I guess it does!" Turning your white-bearded face toward the top of the mountain, you speak in a loud, commanding voice. "I am Hooahtoo. Erupt, oh great Kenalua Volcano! Erupt!"

Turn to PAGE 120.

The creeping figures wear masks that are smaller and plainer than Dr. Oates's. They hand out similar masks to the kneeling workers.

Dr. Oates raises both arms in the air and chants a terrifying rhyme:

> *"The one in the mask*
> *With Tiki Eyes*
> *Gets to decide*
> *Who lives and who dies!"*

You and Gina stare at each other, your eyes wide with fear.

"He's evil!" Gina cries. "We have to get out of here! Now!"

"We have to stop him," you argue. "Who knows what he'll do? And it's our fault. We gave him the eye!"

If you let Gina talk you into running away, turn to PAGE 110.

If you stay to try to stop Dr. Oates, turn to PAGE 114.

You don't know what kind of power the Tiki Eye actually has. But you have to do something!

You reach back to the artifacts table. You grab the first thing your fingers touch. You hold it out in front of you.

An ancient mirror.

"*Aaaaaaiiiiiieeeee!*" Kala shrieks.

Lightning flashes in the sky outside the tent. In a single strike, it bursts through the tent. It hits your mirror, then ricochets off. It knocks Kala to the ground. Before your eyes he shrivels and turns to dust.

All that is left is the sacred Tiki Eye.

Should you grab it?

No. Better not.

Let someone else find out what mysteries lie in the Tiki Eye!

THE END

The horrible creature drags you through the water. It pulls you into another pool-filled cave.

Filled with more giant octopuses!

You don't have time to think! To move! To scream!

All of the monster octopuses wrap their arms around you. The rows of suction cups on each of their arms suck at your skin until it's purple. They grip you so hard, you can barely breathe!

There are too many octopuses to count. And there are definitely too many to escape from. Unless you can wiggle your way out of their tangled mess and leave them tied up in their own knots.

If you think you can wiggle your way out of this tangled octopus maze, turn to PAGE 121.

If you try the escape method you always use when you wrestle with Gina — tickling under the arms — turn to PAGE 48.

134

"You've found the missing Tiki Eye!" Dr. Oates exclaims.

"Tiki Eye?" you repeat. You glance at the stone piece sitting on the towel. The painted eye stares back. You shiver. Something about the stone gives you the creeps.

But Dr. Oates doesn't find the stone scary. He's so happy, he's practically dancing.

"This eye is what our entire archaeological expedition is all about," he gushes. "It's what we've been digging for! All of this effort is to restore the mask to its complete form."

Gina examines the stone. "If this stone is the eye in the mask," Gina asks, "how did the person wearing the mask see? The stone piece is solid."

Dr. Oates beams at her. "Very observant," he comments. "The masks were so large, the eyeholes were lower down. The person wearing the mask would look out the mouth or nose holes."

"What's so special about the mask?" you demand. "Why is it so important to put it back together again?"

Dr. Oates's tone abruptly changes. "Never mind that," he snaps. "The information would mean nothing to you."

Turn to PAGE 97.

Kala presses another button on the throne.

The back wall of the cave rises, and you see the beach. Cheering and whooping, everyone dashes out. You're all free now.

"Thanks to you and Gina, Tiki Island is safe again," Kala says as you walk out together.

"Well, I'm glad it's over," Gina comments.

"Time to start having a real vacation!" you add.

Kala punches you lightly on the arm. "Now maybe you'll take me seriously, instead of thinking I'm always kidding around."

You hang your head sheepishly. "I'm sorry," you apologize. "I should have —"

Kala cuts you off. "Noooo," he murmurs. His face pales. "They're back!" He points a trembling finger at the cave behind you.

"The Tiki warrior spirits?" you gasp. You whirl around.

The cave is empty.

"Gotcha!" Kala laughs so hard, he doubles over. Gina giggles.

You shake your head.

Yup. Everything is back to normal on Tiki Island.

THE END

You and Gina put on your masks. Then you sneak out of the shack.

A group of masked workers surround Oates. "I command you by the Tiki Eye to follow all orders!" he shouts.

"We will follow all orders," the group repeats. They sound like robots. Or zombies.

"Soon Tiki Island will be totally in my control!" Oates cheers. "He who wears the Tiki mask shall rule!"

You glance around the site, trying to come up with a plan. Your eyes land on Dr. Oates's tent. No one is near it. An idea pops into your head.

"Hurry!" you whisper to Gina. "Help me pull down this vine." Together you work quickly and quietly to pull a long vine from a tree.

While Dr. Oates brags about all his power, you and Gina creep over to his tent. You stretch the vine across the entrance to Oates's tent like a rope. Then you and Gina position yourselves on either side of the entrance.

Now all you can do is wait.

Cross your fingers for luck and go to PAGE 123.

You splash into an even bigger pool of clear, still water. Gina flops right beside you.

The waterfall empties into a lake inside another cave. This one is tremendous! The walls are made of pink crystals.

"It's beautiful!" you declare as you gaze around. The entire cave glows pink. Black sand forms a strange, magical beach.

You swim over to a wall. You reach out to touch a pink crystal. It breaks off in your hand. It's sharp, but too beautiful to throw away. You stuff it in your bathing suit to take home.

An earsplitting creaking sound echoes through the cave.

"What was that?" you murmur.

The creaking grows louder and steadier. The blue water turns black. The pink glow becomes bloodred.

Just feet from where you and Gina bob in the water, the ruins of a ship rise up out of the deep pool!

Go to PAGE 54.

About R.L. Stine

R.L. Stine is the most popular author in America. He is the creator of the *Goosebumps*, *Give Yourself Goosebumps*, *Fear Street*, and *Ghosts of Fear Street* series, among other popular books. He has written more than 100 scary novels for kids. Bob lives in New York City with his wife, Jane, teenage son, Matt, and dog, Nadine.